The Same Last Name

D1521669

By Valerie Zahn

The Same Last Name

Prison Book Project
PO Box 592
Titusville, FL 32781

Chapter One

Kat stood in front of the mirror, trying to fix her disheveled appearance. She wished she had concealer to cover the dark circles under her eyes from lack of sleep.

Elaina walked in carrying an arm full of folded towels. "Go ahead and leave to pick up your daughter. This is the last room that needs to be cleaned today. I can handle it."

"Thank you. I owe you one."

"Enjoy your weekend off. Tell Chloe I said hello."

"I will," said Kat.

She put on her coat and rushed out the door to her worn-out gray 2003 Ford Focus. Surprisingly, the engine started on the first try. As she pulled out of the parking lot, she glanced at the gas gauge—nearly empty. She only had thirty dollars in her wallet. It would need to be enough to cover food and entertainment for the weekend with her five-year-old daughter and also food and gas for the beginning of next week. She knew she needed to work more hours at her second job at the Pancake House, but how could she find the time? She already worked every hour she could; she barely had time to sleep.

On her way to get Chloe, Kat drove a little faster than she should have. This was the only semblance of happiness she had felt in two weeks since the last time she'd seen her daughter. The arrangement she had with her ex was a visit every other weekend. Her daughter was the one who kept her going, the reason she got up every single morning and worked herself ragged. Chloe was all she had. She had lost everything in the span of six months. Her man, daughter, home, and comfortable life were gone.

Although she was excited to see Chloe, sadness gripped her as she approached the home that had once been hers. She vividly remembered Justin sitting her down only a few months ago and telling her he had found someone else. That he didn't love her anymore. He had given her a week! Only one week to find somewhere to live, find a job, and move out.

She should have known he would cheat on her. Her mother had never provided much of anything for her, especially words of wisdom, but she *had* said, "Once a cheater, always a cheater."

When they met, she was a server at Craig's Grill and a freshman at MTSU. She went to school during the day and worked there at night and on the weekends. Justin came in regularly and flirted with her. He made her feel special, something she had never felt in her life. He was her knight in shining armor who would rescue her from the terrible life she had always known. He was well off and quite a bit older than her.

The only problem was that he was married.

After only a few months of flirting, he started taking her on dates. He wined and dined her and treated her like a princess. This went on for a few months, and then one night after dinner, she told him she was pregnant with his child. To her surprise, he left and divorced his wife of ten years. He purchased a home of their own, and they lived there for six years. She thought they would grow old together. She also thought they were happy and that their relationship was good until she was told otherwise.

Kat pulled into the driveway of the marble two-story brick and stone house she had once called home. She gripped the steering wheel tightly as memories flooded her, mostly good ones. She noticed the home and driveway had been pressure washed, something she had asked Justin to do dozens of times. Now he had the right motivation, apparently.

But what could Mandy give him that I hadn't? I never held back anything from him. I put my life on hold to have and raise his child. Why wasn't I enough for him? Kat had asked herself these questions thousands of times. She still had no answers.

She sat there for a moment, summoning the courage to get out of the car. After a steadying breath, she forced herself to move.

Mandy's brand-new black BMW sat in the driveway. Kat took another deep breath, smoothed her maid uniform, swallowed any self-esteem she still had, and walked to the front door.

Before she could even ring the doorbell, the door opened and her daughter Chloe was in her arms. "I've missed you so much, Mommy! I've been counting down the days until our next visit. Have you gotten a new job yet? I want to see you more."

"I've missed you too, sweet girl. I haven't found anything else yet. Please don't give up on me. I will. Go and get your things so we can get going."

Chloe ran to her room without a backward glance.

While Kat stood at the entrance, she couldn't help but let her eyes wander. She noticed the new curtains and furniture. Their family portrait that once hung on the wall was replaced with a picture of a magnolia. Christmas decorations were hung everywhere, and not a single one looked familiar.

The smell of a home-cooked meal filled the house. It made her stomach growl. She hadn't eaten since breakfast, and it was now six p.m. Guilt flooded her heart. She hated that Chloe would miss out on a decent meal for fast food from the value menu.

Mandy stepped out of the kitchen and into the living room, wearing an apron and looking like a modern Mrs. Cleaver with her perfect hair and makeup. She looked Kat up and down and gave her a look of pity. "Oh, hi, Kat. Chloe's been missing you. Justin wanted me to tell you to have her back home on Sunday by five. We have a work dinner to attend."

Kat nodded. "At Cynthia's house? She has one every year around this time. Chloe likes to swim in her indoor pool."

Mandy shrugged, a look of aggravation wrinkling her perfect features. "I'm not sure whose house we are going to; honestly, I don't care. Justin wants to introduce me to the people he works with so they can finally put a face to my name."

Chloe walked into the living room with her bag, blanket, and pillow at the same time Justin walked in the door from work. Kat's heart dropped into her stomach. It always hurt so much to see him. She had hoped to be gone before he got home. When they were together, he never got home before six-thirty or seven. She should have known he was fooling around, but love had blinded her.

He walked over and kissed Mandy the way he had once kissed her. He looked so handsome in his light blue button-up shirt and khaki pants. He then walked over to Chloe and kneeled to be eye level with her. "I'm going to miss you, kiddo."

"I will miss you too, Daddy. I wish we could all be together like we used to."

Justin exchanged a glance with Kat. He kissed Chloe on the cheek, and they hugged. "I'll see you in a couple days. Have fun with your mother." Chloe took Kat's hand. "Make sure you have her back here on Sunday—"

"At five, I know. You're going to Cynthia's."

As Kat and Chloe walked out to her car, it took everything in her not to look back at Justin for one more glance. Even though he didn't love her anymore, her heart still ached for him.

Chapter Two

Chloe turned on the radio. 'It's Beginning to Look a Lot like Christmas' was playing. "I love Christmas music, Mommy. Don't you?"

Kat nodded. The truth was, she had only ever liked it when she, Justin, and Chloe were together. Before then, it had only reminded her of what she'd never had—a family.

This year would be the most brutal Christmas she would ever go through. That was saying a lot for someone who had never gotten much of anything for Christmas as a child. She didn't know if Justin would let her even see Chloe that day, or how she would afford any presents for her if he did. She couldn't bear the thought of having any similarities to her mother—someone who had let her down repeatedly.

She could hardly bear listening to the music as the words rang out, "I'll Be Home for Christmas." She reached over and turned it off.

"Why did you turn off the music, Mommy?"

"Let's talk instead."

"Do you have any decorations up?"

"No, sweetheart, I don't. I'm sorry. I know you love them so much. I can't afford to buy much of anything extra right now. It won't always be that way, though."

"It's okay. I brought markers, crayons, and paper. I'll make you some."

"I would love that. Your decorations are my favorite ones."

As they turned into a neighborhood on the other side of town, Chloe asked, "Have I been here before, Mommy?"

"Yes, this is the same place you came to for our last visit. Unfortunately, I can't afford anything better right now."

"Do you ever get scared living here?"

"Sometimes, but I lived in similar kinds of neighborhoods growing up with my mom. It's not so bad. At least I have a roof over my head, and I'm not still sleeping on Elaina's couch. Don't tell your daddy how bad it is, or he won't let you come visit me."

"Why don't you ask Daddy for money? He has lots of it. He buys things for Mandy all the time."

Kat felt a pang in her heart. Justin had given her jewelry and expensive trinkets too earlier in their relationship. "Your daddy is why I had to move in the first place. He doesn't love me anymore. He would never give me money, and I would never ask."

Chloe's face fell. "What if Daddy stops loving me like he did you?"

"That's never going to happen, sweetheart. It's impossible to stop loving your child."

"But you didn't have a daddy growing up, and your mommy didn't care about you?"

Kat held her breath for a second while trying not to show emotion. "Well, that's me. That's not you. Your mommy and daddy love you very much, even if we aren't together anymore."

When she parked her car, she sat there for a minute trying to figure out how to prepare her daughter for the considerable contrast of living conditions she was used to. Even though she had been there before, it was still an adjustment.

"Why aren't we going inside, Mommy?"

"We will still be sleeping on the couch together. I haven't been able to get a bed yet."

"Is it the same couch you got from the trash?"

"It wasn't from the trash. Someone put it out on their curb to get rid of it."

Chloe gave her a sarcastic look. "That's the trash, Mommy."

"At least the price was right."

"So, are we going to go in?"

Kat reluctantly got out of the car and helped Chloe out. When they walked in, Chole looked around the small one-bedroom duplex. It looked the same as the last time she was there. It was dark, with painted cinderblock walls. The carpet was so worn out that it exposed the concrete beneath it. There were no curtains, table, or chairs—only a dirty, worn-out couch, small stove, and refrigerator. The dampness in the air made it feel chilly, matching the scenery.

Chloe walked over to her mother and hugged her legs.

"What's that for?"

"I'm sorry you have to live here, Mommy. One day, I'm going to get a good job and buy you a better house."

Guilt clenched her gut. She'd started working as soon as she was old enough so she and her mother could survive. She hadn't minded because it allowed her to escape her mother and her many boyfriends. "It's okay, sweetheart. It's good enough for me." She kneeled to eye-level and kissed Chloe's cheek. Justin's cologne lingered where he had kissed her goodbye earlier. Tears instantly filled Kat's eyes.

"Why are you crying, Mommy?"

"It's just… I have missed you so much, and I'm thrilled you are here." Chloe hugged her mother tightly. "You can put your things over there by the couch. I forgot to grab your food from the car. I will get it and be right back."

"Why didn't you get any food, Mommy?"

"I told you already; I ate before I picked you up. I'm not hungry. I will finish up whatever you don't want."

"I wish you had a TV."

"So do I. Maybe I'll have one the next time you come."

"You said that last time."

"I'll tell you what; after you eat, we'll walk to the park or the library."

"Walk?"

"Yeah, I don't have much gas in the car, so we'll be doing a lot of walking this weekend. It will be like an adventure. We can run or walk slowly. We can pretend like we are animals in the wild."

Chloe giggled with excitement. "I'll be a unicorn."

Kat smiled and kissed her on the cheek. "I'll be right back."

As Kat walked out to the car to get the fast food, guilt pricked her. Maybe if she had been good enough for Justin, he would have never looked for someone else. She had never been good enough for anyone. What was wrong with her? Why did all the people in her life only use her for what they wanted and then dispose of her when she had nothing left to offer? Perhaps one day, Chloe would realize she didn't need her either and never want to see her again.

Before entering the duplex, Kat wiped the tears from her eyes and took a deep breath.

⁓⸎⁓

As they were walking home from the park, Chloe began slowing the pace. "I'm so tired, Mommy. I'm tired of this adventure. I don't want to walk anymore."

Kat knew if she got her mind off walking, she would forget how tired she was. "When we get home, I'll read a book we got from the library today. Do you want to read the one about the dog or the unicorn first?"

"The unicorn!"

"That's what I thought you would say."

"Mandy reads a story to me every night before bed. She says that one day she's going to be my mommy. She's nice, but she's not you. I don't know why Daddy wanted her more than you."

Kat's eye stung, and she tried her best to mask her feelings. She had plenty of time to cry when Chloe wasn't there. She had cried buckets over the past few months. Besides, Justin would never marry Mandy. He and Kat had been together for six years—she'd even had his child—and he had never asked her to marry him. She had dreamed that he would so all of them could have the same last name. But that day hadn't come, and by the way things looked now, it never would.

An hour later, Kat covered Chloe up with her blanket and kissed her on the forehead. She turned out the light and then lay down at the other end of the couch. "Goodnight, sweetheart."

"Good night, Mommy."

After a few minutes, she heard Chloe crying and sat up. "What's wrong? Do you want to talk about it?"

"I don't want you to take me home tomorrow. I'll miss you too much."

Kat's heart ached. How could she tell her daughter that she was the only reason for getting out of bed each morning? She was the only thing in her life that gave her any joy. "I will miss you too. More than you know. But since we can't change anything right now, why not think about the things you look forward to when you get home tomorrow?"

Chloe sniffled and then was quiet for a few minutes. "I look forward to seeing Daddy and sleeping in my own bed. I miss my toys, snacks, and the kind of food I like."

Tears streamed down Kat's face as Chloe described the things she couldn't give her. She was thankful Chloe couldn't see her in the dark room. She was doing her best to survive, but her daughter deserved so much more than she could ever provide for her. Perhaps Chloe would be better off if she were dead and gone. Then she wouldn't feel torn between her and Justin. At least when she was with Justin, she had everything she needed. Kat worked anywhere from thirteen to fifteen hours a day and could barely afford rent, gas, cell phone, and enough food for herself.

Hopelessness clutched her. She would never be able to provide for Chloe.

She didn't sleep at all that night as she cried and watched her daughter sleep peacefully beside her.

Chapter Three

Chloe didn't say much on the way home. Kat could see her little mind mulling something over. "Are you okay, sweetheart? You barely touched your breakfast or lunch and you've been very quiet."

"Yes, I just have mixed-up feelings. I'm excited to get back home and see Daddy and my toys, but I'll miss you too much. Sometimes I accidentally call Mandy mommy. I think she likes it, but I hate when I do it."

"I'm so sorry you've been put in this situation. It's not fair," said Kat.

"It's not fair to you either, Mommy."

Kat said nothing—mainly because what she wanted to say was entirely inappropriate for a five-year-old to hear.

When they pulled into the driveway and parked, Chloe unbuckled her seat belt, put her arms around her mother's neck, and held her tightly. "I don't want you to go, Mommy. I want you to stay and for things to be like they used to be."

Tears filled Kat's eyes. "So do I, sweetheart, but we both know I can't stay. You have to be brave now and go inside. We'll see each other again soon. I'll keep working hard, and I'll eventually get a better job and home. Then I can hire a lawyer, and then, who knows? Maybe we'll be able to see each other every week."

Chloe didn't say anything. She just kept holding on and crying.

"Hey, aren't you going to Cynthia's today? You will get to go swimming. You love to swim."

Chloe let go and wiped her tears, and they slowly got out of the car.

As soon as they walked into the house, Justin picked Chloe up. "I missed you, kiddo. Did you have fun?"

Chloe just nodded.

Mandy walked out of the kitchen, beaming. "Look, Chloe!" she said as she lifted her left hand. A colossal princess-cut diamond ring shone on her finger. "Your daddy and I are engaged! I'm going to be your stepmom officially."

Kat's heart stopped, and she met Justin's gaze. Her legs felt weak, and her stomach felt sick.

Chloe, clearly noticing the hurt in her mother's eyes, walked over and hugged her around the legs.

"We need to get going, Chloe. Go and put your bathing suit on under your clothes so we can leave," said Justin.

Chloe obeyed, but looked back at her mother as she walked to her room.

Kat summoned every ounce of strength she could and asked, "When is the big day?"

"June 11th. I have so much to do between now and then," said Mandy, obviously overjoyed.

"Congratulations on your engagement. Please tell Cynthia I said hello." Determined not to let them see her cry, she turned and walked out, holding her breath.

While walking back to her car, it took every ounce of strength in her to breathe again. She had been through a lot in her life, but her heart had never felt so broken as it did at that moment. Why did everyone in her life always discard her as trash? She'd never once been truly loved or wanted.

Kat started her car. The engine stalled and died. She tried again, and luckily it started this time.

Why would Justin propose to Mandy when he never did to her? Mandy would have everything Kat wanted. Her man, her daughter, and they would share the same last name.

She had ten dollars in her purse. She knew it should be used to buy gas or food, but instead, she found herself at Allen's Bar. That ten dollars wouldn't get her drunk, but hopefully her good looks—which as a child had felt more like a curse—would prompt someone to buy her a few drinks.

Being here made her hate herself even more. She'd never wanted to be like her mother by numbing her problems with booze. But how else could she deal with the misery festering inside her like an incurable infection?

A familiar feeling swelled inside her as she looked around the crowded bar.

Loneliness.

The longer she sat there, the more she thought about her life. She was a mistake. She should never have been born. She could no longer bear the thought of waking up to another day and feeling the same anguish, sorrow, and hopelessness. The feeling that she had no one who loved her unconditionally, other than her daughter, was unbearable. She had no hope of things ever changing. It went as far back in her childhood as she could remember.

Kat never knew her father; he left when her mother told him she was pregnant. She was placed in foster care when she was four years old, and her mom got her back just before her fifth birthday. This pattern went on for several years. She would finally settle into a home and think she had some permanency, her mother would do just enough to get her back, and the vicious cycle would start all over again.

Finally, when she was eleven years old and somewhat old enough to take care of her mother, she hid her living conditions from her teachers and other adults so she wouldn't be taken into state custody again. Not because she wanted to be with her mother, but because she couldn't take the heartbreak of leaving another decent home and family to return to the unstable misery she was bound to. It wasn't uncommon for her to clean up her mother's urine or vomit almost nightly, or to fight off the attention from men her mother brought home. She still remembered the stench of liquor and vomit on their breath.

Hopelessness settled in her heart like a heavy weight. She took a piece of paper and pen from her purse and began writing a letter to the only person who had ever truly loved her.

Chloe,

I love you more than anything in this world. You have always been my little ray of sunshine and the brightest light in my life. I'm sorry that I left you. You may not understand it now, but you will be better off without me. I am only an anchor that would have eventually held you down. Your father and everyone else in my life figured that out. You would have, too. Now you won't feel torn between your daddy and me. You won't feel the need to ever take care of me.

You are a special little girl. I know you will make a difference in this big world by just being you. I love you, sweetheart, more than anything.

Love,

Mommy

Kat folded the letter and put it under her empty glass and her last ten dollars. Then she got up and walked outside, ready for her opportunity to end her torment forever.

Chapter Four

Nathan was on his fourth day on the job as a barback. He looked at his watch, relieved that his shift would be over in ten minutes. As he was wiping down the counter, he noticed the woman sitting there had left while he was in the restroom. Unhappiness was a familiar look on the faces of most of the people who came in there. However, this lady had a look beyond unhappiness—more like despair. He'd tried to talk to her a few times, but her mind had seemed entirely elsewhere.

Nathan picked up her glass to wipe the counter and noticed a ten-dollar bill and a folded-up piece of paper underneath it. He was reluctant at first to open it, but he did. As soon as he read it, he ran out from behind the counter and out of the bar.

His heart raced wildly as he searched the parking lot. "Lord, please," he muttered. "I know that You have me here for a reason. Show me where she is and how I can help her." He squinted from the bright headlights that flashed in his eyes. Then he saw the woman standing by the curb of the busy street. The blinding lights of a large semi-truck were only a few yards away from her, and she was anxiously waiting for it.

Nathan began running as fast as he could. He made it to her seconds before the truck would have hit her. Car horns blared as he tackled her out of harm's way.

The woman started screaming, kicking, and crying while hitting him with both arms. He stood there, allowing his six-three frame to take every blow, not saying anything.

It took several minutes before the woman got a little control of herself. She sat down on the side of the road, holding her knees pressed against her chest, her head buried in them, sobbing.

Nathan held back tears as he was moved with compassion for her. He watched as her dark brown hair blew in the cold night air. She was a little younger than him and beautiful. What was so bad in her life that would make her want to end it? Not knowing what to do, he sat beside her on the curb and remained silent until she was ready to talk.

After about half an hour, he put his hand on her shoulder. "Would you like to get some coffee and talk?"

She looked up at him with mascara streaked down both cheeks. Her swollen, dark brown eyes glared at him.

"I don't have a dime in my pocket. I don't know if I even have enough gas in my car to get home. Please, just leave me alone."

"I'm paying. I won't leave you alone like this."

"I said, leave me alone!"

"You can either come with me, or I can call the police to get you some help."

"Are you threatening me?" she asked with a stern tone.

"No, but I won't let you end your life on my watch." He stood and offered his hand to help her up. She didn't take it and got up on her own.

They crossed the busy street, and she followed him to his car. He opened the door for her, and she gave him a strange look. "I'm not helpless. I can open a door."

"I'm sure you can. But my mother taught me always to open the door for a lady."

"I'm sure if your mother knew me, she would make an exception."

"Oh, you are definitely wrong about that. My mom could relate to any woman hurting and in trouble." The woman glanced his way, as if she wanted to hear more. "See, my dad was killed in a car accident when I was four. He was the breadwinner in the family. My mom became a single mom and the sole provider for us in a single moment."

Nathan had her full attention now. "What did she do? How did things turn out for her?"

"Well, she clung to her faith and worked hard. Over time, things got a little easier and better. She eventually met and married a nice man and had two more children."

They pulled up to a small twenty-four-hour diner. Kat sat there a moment, perhaps thinking about what he had said. He didn't know her situation, but he hoped his words brought her some hope.

Nathan got out of the car and opened her door. As they walked in, Kat's arms were crossed, and her demeanor was guarded. When they sat down, a waitress handed each of them a menu covered in grease residue. Her eyes widened as she looked at the woman across from Nathan. "Has anyone ever told you that you look like—"

"Jessica Alba?" She nodded. "I get it all the time."

"You could be her sister."

Kat sighed. "I wish I were. I would give anything to have a different life than mine."

"What can I get you to drink?"

Nathan looked at the woman. "Get whatever you want."

"All I want is coffee." She handed the menu back to the waitress.

"And for you?"

He usually wouldn't have caffeine so late, but he suspected this would be a long night. "I'll have coffee, too. Thank you."

"Two coffees, coming right up," said the waitress as she walked to the counter.

"My name is Nathan, by the way."

"You can call me Kat."

"Kat." He remembered it from the letter she'd left on the counter. "Is that a nickname or an abbreviation of your name?"

"My name is Katarina. I was named after my grandmother. It's the only thing my family ever gave me."

The waitress brought their coffee and a small bowl with packs of sugar and creamer. "Thank you," they both said in unison.

After a long silence, Nathan asked, "Do you have any family, Kat?"

"Only my daughter. My mom was an alcoholic. She died five years ago. My dad left her when she told him she was pregnant with me. I was in and out of foster care for most of my childhood. I thought I had friends until my ex cheated on me and kicked me out of our home of six years. Those so-called friends disappeared the moment I had nothing. I now have one friend, Elaina. We met in one of the foster homes I lived in for a while. She got adopted by a single mom who saw her more as a babysitter than a daughter, and I was given back to my mother, who had changed only enough to get me back. After that, she went back to her normal no-good self. I kept to myself growing up and didn't make any friends in school. I did everything I could to stay out of state custody. I would have been instantly taken if anyone knew my living conditions."

"Are you from here?"

"I was born in Florida. We lived in Alabama, Georgia, Illinois, and now in Tennessee. My mom moved every time I got out of custody except for the last time. It didn't matter where we moved to; she always seemed to find the bars and the same kind of friends."

"So, you have your daughter Chloe and your friend Eliana?"

Kat's dark eyes widened. "How do you know her name?" she asked with panic in her voice.

"I read your suicide letter."

Kat stared at the man she'd only just met as he pulled her suicide letter out of his pocket.

"Here it is, by the way."

She snatched it from his hand and sighed in frustration. "You weren't supposed to read that."

"Well, I'm glad I did. You've obviously had a hard life. But what happened recently to make you want to give it up and leave your daughter?"

"Over the last six months, I've lost everything. My ex moved his new girlfriend into our home. She lives with my daughter, while I live in a crappy apartment. I'm working two jobs and as many hours as I can, and I can barely afford to survive, let alone ever be able to support my daughter."

"Please keep your voice down. People are looking at us."

"I'm sorry. What can I say? I'm angry. What makes me the angriest is that I was with Justin for over six years. I even had his child. He never asked me to marry him. I never had my mom's last name or the foster families I lived with. Even though he knew how badly I wanted us all to have the same last name, he never made it happen. This afternoon, after taking my daughter back to the house I used to call home, Mandy showed off her enormous diamond engagement ring. They are getting married in six months." She began to cry again.

"I'm really sorry. I can't imagine how hard this must be on you."

Kat wiped her face. She couldn't believe she was telling a stranger her life story. She usually guarded herself against everyone. "I don't need your pity, Nathan. Enough about me. What's your story?"

"I get the last name thing bothering you. After my mom remarried, she took my stepdad's last name. When he adopted me, he gave me the option of taking his name. I didn't because it was the only thing I had left of my real dad. So even now, I'm the only Spencer in my immediate family."

Her lips curved into a half smile, "So you do get it. That feeling of being left out and not fully belonging. At least you have the name of someone who loved and wanted you, not one who bailed after finding out you existed." She sighed. "Sorry to be such a downer. I'm not usually like this. Tell me more about yourself, Nathan Spencer."

"Well, I am a pastor at New Life Hope church just down the street."

"What?" She laughed. "That's a good one."

"I'm serious."

"You are a bad liar. I saw you working at the bar."

"Yes. I started working there because Jesus said to go and make disciples. I don't feel God wants me to wait for people to attend church. He wants me to go out and get people to come."

"Oh, so I see what this is all about. You are trying to convert me. Well, you're wasting your time. God never had anything to do with me. I won't waste my time on Him."

"I'm not trying to convert you. I can't convert anyone. I only want to help you."

"Help me?" She laughed. "Can you get me a better job? A better place to live? Can you help me get my daughter and ex back?"

He rubbed his chin, thinking. "I can probably help you get a better job and place to live. That could help you get your daughter. Concerning your ex, I can't help you there."

She looked him over. He was nice-looking; tall, with a muscular build, dark hair, and deep blue eyes. He had a nice haircut, and she liked how he dressed. He wore a plaid shirt over a tight-fitting white T-shirt and jeans. "Are you married or seeing anyone?"

"No."

She wondered why someone like him was single? He must have a weird personality or some major emotional flaw. It would come out eventually, but what did it matter? Justin wouldn't know. "I think there is a way you could help me get my ex back."

"Okay. How?"

"You are a nice-looking man. If he thought we were dating, he might get jealous and want me back. Of course, we wouldn't be. We would only be pretending."

He laughed. "You want me to pretend to date you."

"It's only for six months and would be completely platonic."

"You, too, are nice-looking. Why me? I'm sure you could easily find someone else."

"You seem nice, and you said you wanted to help. It's only six months or less. By then, he will either be married or back with me."

"With his track record, he may be with someone else," said Nathan.

She shrugged. "So, will you?"

He sat there, thinking it over for a minute. "I won't lie. I'll promise to exclusively date you for the next six months or until he tries to get you back, whichever comes first. However, you have to do some things for me as well."

"Okay. What do you want?" she asked with hesitation.

"I will gladly help you with your job and apartment, but please take out that suicide letter and turn it over and write down what you'll have to do for me."

She took the letter she had stuffed into her purse, smoothed it out, turned it over, and got her pen in her hand, ready to write.

"For the next six months, I want you to open your blinds or curtains every morning and let the sunshine in. Then thank God for at least five things you are grateful for."

She stopped writing and gave him a puzzled look. His expression didn't change, so she continued writing.

"I want you to read at least one chapter in the Bible every day, starting in the book of Luke."

"I don't have a Bible."

"We can easily take care of that. I also want you to go with me to church every Sunday that you can. Lastly, I want you to get counseling."

She stopped writing and put her pen down. "I'm not going to counseling."

"Shh, keep your voice down. Listen, if I reported what you did tonight, you would be in a mental hospital right now. You need counseling. We provide counseling at our church. It's completely confidential, and it's free."

"You are asking a lot from me, Nathan." She broke eye contact. "But I'm asking a lot from you too. Okay, I'll do it."

He reached into his pocket and pulled out a wad of cash. "Here are my tips for the night. Hopefully this will cover your gas and food until you get your next paycheck."

"I can't take your money."

"Please, I want you to have it."

She pushed his hand away and shook her head emphatically.

"You can pay me back when you get on your feet."

She rolled her eyes. She was embarrassed to take it, but she knew she had no choice, so she reluctantly plucked it from his outstretched hand.

"What time do you get off tomorrow?" Nathan asked.

"I don't get off until five from my first job. I start the other one at six. I don't get off from that one until eleven. That's if they don't need me to stay longer."

"You must be exhausted." He grabbed a napkin from the napkin holder. "Write down your address on this."

She paused for a second, wondering if she should trust him. Realizing she had nothing to lose, she wrote it down and handed it back to him.

"I'll pick you up at your place tomorrow night at eleven thirty. We'll have a quick dinner or, in my case, a light snack."

She blinked hard. "Why are you doing all this for me?"

He shrugged. "I'm a Christian. Showing unselfish concern for people is what I'm supposed to do. In saying that, what's your favorite color?"

"Purple. Why?"

"You'll find out tomorrow."

"Since you're going to find me a better job, I'll call out tomorrow for my job at the Pancake House. You can pick me up at five thirty instead."

He grinned. "I like your confidence."

They barely spoke on the way back to the bar. When he parked, she looked over at him. "Don't get out. I can handle my door. Are you sure you want to do this? After all, I'm a stranger. There are easier ways to get people to come to your church."

He laughed. "I'm sure there are. The question is, do *you* want to do this?"

Her mouth tightened, "I'll do anything to get my daughter and old life back. So yes, I'm all in."

He gave a single nod of approval. "Then I'll see you tomorrow."

Chapter Five

The next day, Kat stretched as she slowly got up from her couch. Her back ached from the lack of support from the thin, worn cushions, and her head throbbed from all the crying the night before. But she remembered her promise and walked over to the window. She had been embarrassed to tell him she didn't have curtains or blinds because she couldn't afford them.

Kat stared out the window toward the duplex behind hers. It looked like it should be condemned. A few children were walking out to catch their school bus. Her heart hurt for them. She remembered being made fun of for the different places she'd lived in as a child. She was thankful Chloe didn't have to live in her duplex permanently.

Her conversation with Nathan returned to her. What were five things that she could be thankful for? She thought about it for a second. Halfheartedly, she said, "I know I'm not on your favorite list, and you don't care much for me. But I made a promise to Nathan, so here goes. Thank you for my daughter Chloe. She's everything to me. Thank you for my friend Elaina. Thank you that I have a place to call home. Thank you for giving me another chance to make a better life. How many is that?" She counted on her fingers. "Four. Oh, and thank you that I have money to put gas in my car today. Amen."

She looked at the time on her phone. She had fifteen minutes before she needed to leave for work, so she quickly got ready and headed out the door.

When she turned the ignition, her car wouldn't start. She tried again, but nothing. A third time—still nothing. With a sigh, she picked up her phone and called her only friend. "Elaina, can you please come by and pick me up? My car won't start. Thanks."

She tried to start the car one more time with no success, then went back inside to warm up while she waited for Elaina to arrive.

Fifteen minutes later, Elaina pulled in, and Kat ran out and got into her car.

"Now we're both going to be late," said Elaina.

"I'm so sorry. If I had anyone else to call, I would have."

"No, it's okay. I'm glad you called and that I could help. How was your weekend with Chloe?"

Kat let out a deep sigh. "My time with her was wonderful, as always. It was everything else that made it... well... horrible."

When they stopped at a red light, Elaina got a better look at Kat. "You look terrible. Were you up crying all night again?"

"Not all night."

"Was it because you saw Justin and...?"

"Mandy showed off her new engagement ring when I dropped Chloe off. They're getting married in June."

"What? Oh, I'm so sorry."

"That isn't the worst of it. I was so distraught after I found out that I... I almost took my own life. If the barback at Allen's hadn't stopped me, I wouldn't be here right now."

Elaina gasped and swerved a little, almost hitting the car next to them. "Kat Baker! How could you! What about Chloe? What about me?"

"Honestly, you both would be better off without me."

"Stop talking like that! We have to stick together. Why didn't you call me?"

"It was really late. I didn't want to wake you or the kids. Besides, I talked to Nathan. He's supposedly going to help me. He's a pastor at a church around here. He's taking me to dinner after I get off. I'm not working at the

Pancake House tonight. I've already called in, which is a good thing since my car won't start."

"Wait, did you say Nathan was a barback or a pastor?"

"He's both."

Elaina laughed.

"I laughed too when I found out. He says he works at the bar to invite people to church. It's crazy, right? I know he's going to try to convert me, but..."

They both laughed.

"Well, take the help where you can get it," Elaina said. "God knows you can use it. But we both know he'll never be able to change you."

At five-thirty sharp, there was a knock on her door. Kat scrambled to answer it. She didn't want to invite him in, so she grabbed her purse and turned off the lights so he couldn't see how bad her apartment was. Then she cracked open the door. "Okay, let's go."

He laughed as she walked quickly to his car. "Well, okay then. Are you that hungry?"

"It's been a long day," said Kat. He walked around and opened her door. She rolled her eyes and got inside. "You don't have to keep opening doors for me. It's not like your mother's here."

"We're seeing one another now, so you better get used to it. It comes with the package." He got behind the wheel and started the car.

He couldn't help but notice how attractive she was. She had shoulder-length brown hair, dark brown eyes, and a natural tan. He couldn't understand how a man could drop her so easily for someone else, especially after having his child. Her eyes were still swollen from the crying the night before. She also had dark circles around them. He assumed it was due to a lack of sleep from the stress and working so much. He genuinely felt sorry for her and was determined to help her however he could.

"If it's okay, we'll stop by the church before dinner. I want to introduce you to Linda. She'll be your counselor over the next few months."

Kat sighed in aggravation.

"It's part of the arrangement, remember?"

"I know. I just dread talking to a stranger about personal things in my life." She gave a sheepish smile. "I know it sounds weird because I poured out my guts to you last night, but that's not the norm for me. Maybe I was a little tipsy, or maybe it was the adrenaline from almost getting hit by a semi-truck. Besides, it's not like it will help."

"There's nothing you can tell her that will surprise her. She's been doing this for years. Counseling does help. I went to her for a couple years."

"What could you possibly need counseling for?"

"I told you about my dad dying in a car accident when I was four. My stepdad didn't come into the picture until I was ten. Even though I wanted a father figure, I wanted my dad, not a replacement. That in itself caused issues that needed to be dealt with. There's no human alive who doesn't have some type of issue. It's nice to talk to someone sometimes to help you sort out your emotions and your past."

"I'm sorry—you're right. I'm sure that was very hard for you. I can't believe I almost did something similar to my daughter last night, and it wouldn't have been an accident, but entirely my fault. Thanks to you, I didn't."

"Thanks to God you didn't. I believe He had me there for a reason—you."

She rolled her eyes but didn't contradict him. Luckily, he didn't bring up God again.

They pulled into the church parking lot, and she was relieved to see that only a few other cars were there. Nathan opened her door and helped her out.

As soon as she walked through the doors, the familiar smell of the church brought back memories. She hadn't been inside one since she was ten years old, with one of the foster families. It was right before her mom got her back for the last time. She was hoping to get married in a church, but that day never came.

As they walked down the narrow halls, she saw a sign that said, "Jesus Loves You."

If Jesus loves me, where has He been all my life? Was He there the multiple nights I cleaned my mother's vomit off the couch? Where was He when my innocence was taken from me by different men my mother brought home? Where was He when Justin kicked me out and I lost everything? He may love good people, but He doesn't love me.

Nathan knocked on a door. A short, petite-framed woman with curly brown hair and kind eyes opened it. "Nathan!" She hugged him. "Is this Kat?"

Kat gave a half smile. "Yes."

"Hi, I'm Linda." She reached out her hand, and Kat shook it. "Nathan informed me earlier that you need some counseling."

Kat's mouth tightened. *I don't need counseling,* she thought, but she didn't say anything. "Well, what weekday is good for you? I can work with your schedule."

"I don't get off work most days until eleven at night. My days off are pretty random. I could try to get off every Monday from my second job. I get off from my day job around five."

"All right then, we'll meet on Mondays around five-thirty. Does that sound good to you?"

She shrugged. "Sure. I won't need counseling for long. Only a few months."

Linda smiled and exchanged a glance with Nathan. "You can come for as long as you need. There's no pressure. I'm here only to help."

"We should be going," Nathan said. "We stopped by on our way to dinner."

Linda reached out her hand again. "It's nice meeting you, Kat. I look forward to getting to know you better. I'll see you next week."

Kat smiled and then followed Nathan back down the hall.

"Before we go, I want to show you the sanctuary, so you'll know where to come on Sunday."

She sighed. She'd forgotten that she promised to go to church every Sunday.

They walked through the double doors. This church was huge. It seemed much more modern than the one she attended as a child. That church had blue carpet and wooden pews instead of comfy padded theater seats. Hopefully that didn't mean the sermons were long.

She rubbed the back of a few seats as she walked down the aisle. Unwanted memories flooded her thoughts.

"What are you thinking about?" asked Nathan.

"The last time I was in church."

"Do you want to talk about it?"

"Not really. It wasn't a good experience. It's one of the reasons I've never wanted to come back."

"Let me ask you a question. If you went to a bad hair stylist, would you ever get your hair cut again?"

"Of course. If not, my hair would look like Rapunzel. I would just go to a different one."

"Right. I don't think it's good to church hop, but I do know that every church out there isn't teaching the things they should—also, people like different things such as crowd size, music, and preaching. There's no such thing as a perfect church, but one should find a church that best fits them or their family. So instead of completely not going, you should find another one."

She shrugged. "I don't think church in itself is a good match for me."

"Oh, I almost forgot. I have something for you. Come with me to my office."

They walked out the double doors and down another narrow hallway. Nathan opened the door to a small, tidy office. It had a desk and a couple of chairs across from it. There was a computer and papers stacked perfectly beside the keyboard. He pulled out a drawer, took out a small box, and handed it to her. "This is for you."

"For me?" She opened it and couldn't keep from smiling. She slowly opened the box. It was the most beautiful Bible she had ever seen. It was purple, with darker purple flowers perfectly placed on the cover. There, in silver, was engraved *Katarina*. She rubbed her name with her thumb. She had never been given anything so personal. As much as she didn't want to be happy about a Bible, she was. Her guard lowered for a brief moment. "Thank you."

"You're welcome. There's space left beside your name. Maybe when you and Justin get back together, you can put your new last name there."

Kat smiled. She liked the sound of that. She opened the Bible and noticed a bookmark at the beginning of the book of Luke. She flipped through it. "These chapters are so long. You can't expect me to read an entire chapter every night."

"Okay. Instead of reading a chapter, how about reading one section a day?"

"That sounds more reasonable."

"Good. Are you ready to get some dinner?"

"I've been ready for a while," she said as she put the Bible back in the box.

"Then let's go," said Nathan, holding the door open for her.

Chapter Six

K at sighed as she turned off the alarm on her phone. Her gut clenched when she realized it was Sunday.

Thanks to Nathan, her car was fixed. After looking it over, he found it was only her battery, and he bought a new one and replaced it in less than an hour. The thought of her IOU list made her pulse kick up a notch. When she got a better job, she intended to pay him back every penny he had spent on her.

The only problem she needed to focus on now was that she didn't have an excuse to miss church.

She reluctantly got up, then went to her closet. Her clothes, her lousy car, Chloe, and a broken heart were the only things she still had left from her relationship with Justin. However, as heartbroken as she was, she would do it all over again to have Chloe in her life.

While she showered and got ready, dread overwhelmed her. She could hardly bear the thought of the stares when she walked into the church. Or how the pastor would preach directly at her as if he could see into her soul. She wished Nathan would be preaching. At least he already knew how wretched she was. But he had mentioned over dinner that he was the connection pastor. His job was to get new people to come to church and get them plugged in, whatever that meant. He was obviously good at his job. Other than for her dream wedding, she had never wanted to step foot into another church, and now she was going because of him.

As she started her car, she remembered she hadn't listed the five things she was grateful for today. She wasn't a good person by any stretch of the imagination, but she refused to be a liar. Most of her life had been spent surrounded by liars. Her mother was a liar, and everyone she had kept company with. Kat was determined never to be like them.

"God, thank you for Chloe. Thank you that my car started this morning. Thank you for the nice clothes to wear. Thank you for a place to live. Thank you for food."

After she finished, she found herself smiling. Maybe there was something to this being thankful thing.

As she approached the church, her smile dwindled to a frown. Nervousness settled in her stomach. Why was she so scared? She didn't care what people thought about her. It felt almost as hard to go there as it was to go back to her old house where Justin and Mandy lived.

The parking lot was packed full. This was the service with the smallest crowd? Good thing she was coming to this one and not the eleven o'clock service.

Kat parked the car and remained there for a moment, watching all the happy families walking in together. Their smiling faces ignited fury in her. She wanted to leave, but she couldn't. She had given her word, and Nathan had kept his side of their arrangement so far.

Her heart pounded so hard that she worried people would hear it. Seeing all the happy families made her feel even more alone. She felt like a spotlight was following her as she walked hesitantly into the church.

Apparently, Nathan had been watching for her, because he came straight over before she had even seen him. His excitement at seeing her was refreshing. Not only was he a familiar face, but a nonjudgmental one.

His smile faded when he got a good look at her. "What's wrong?"

"I feel like everyone is staring at me."

"You're new. They want to meet you and get to know you."

"I don't want to meet or know them. If I had my way, I would turn around, walk out of here, and never come back."

"That will change."

She rolled her eyes. "You don't know me very well."

"That, too, will change," he said, his smile returning.

A lovely looking couple walked up to them. "Hi, Nathan."

"Oh, hey, let me introduce you to Katarina."

Kat's neck turned so quickly to Nathan that she felt like she had whiplash.

The lady reached out her hand. "Hi, Katarina. My name is Ann."

Kat shook her hand. "You can call me Kat."

Just then, the worship team leader greeted the congregation. Nathan and Kat quickly went to their seats, where she leaned over and whispered, "Why did you introduce me as Katarina?"

"Because that's your name, and that's what I'll call you from now on."

"Everyone calls me Kat."

"I don't care what other people call you. I'm going to call you by your birth name." "Why?"

"I'll tell you one day."

She sighed and rolled her eyes. When the music started, she was surprised at the upbeat and modern tempo. She would never admit it, but she liked it.

When the worship time was over, Kat's stomach churned. She knew what came next: the sermon. The sermon would remind her she was a terrible person, that God was out to get her, and that she would one day rot in hell. She was determined to ignore all of it. But as hard as she tried, she couldn't. She listened to every single word. To her surprise, it wasn't condemning—it was about love and how we are to love others.

This must be why Nathan was the way he was. He had demonstrated every attribute the pastor spoke of to her, a mere stranger. She felt fortunate she had met him.

When the sermon was over, relief rushed over her. She had survived it. She still had several more sermons to endure, but she was hopeful that Justin would soon get jealous and want her back. Or maybe, with it being winter, she would get a cold and be able to miss a few. But at least she was down one, and next week she would feel less alone because Chloe would be with her.

After the sermon, Nathan took her hand. "I want to introduce you to a family. Come with me."

The way he said it was like she had a choice, but how he pulled her along made her feel otherwise. He walked her over to an attractive couple who looked to be in their late fifties or early sixties and were finishing up a conversation with another couple. Huge smiles were on everyone's faces. Why did people seem so happy here? Was it real or a façade?

One of the couples excused themselves. "Hey, Nathan! It's so good to see you."

Nathan reached out and shook both of their hands. "Hey, Mike and Cindy. I want to introduce you to my friend Katarina."

Kat held back her frustration as he said her full name. She shook both of their hands when they reached out.

"Katarina has been through a lot over the past several months. She is in a tough spot and needs a better job and home. She is a hard worker and works as a maid at the Abbington Hotel during the day and as a waitress at the Pancake House in the evenings. I was wondering if you had any jobs available at the apartment complex?"

Heat rushed to her cheeks. Did he just come out and say that? Was he literally asking them to give her a job right in front of her?

"As a matter of fact, we do. We need an assistant office manager. We can discuss pay later; I'm sure it would be more than you're making now, and you wouldn't have to pay rent. It also comes with a furnished apartment. Your responsibilities would be covering the office and showing people apartments that are available. Do you think you would be interested?"

Kat's eyes widened in disbelief. She tried to say something, but words wouldn't come out at first. After a stunned moment, she managed, "Yes, absolutely."

"When can you come by and fill out the paperwork for the job?"

"I'm off tomorrow."

"Perfect! Come by whenever. One of us should be there." The man reached out his hand, and they shook again.

"Thank you!"

He nodded and patted Nathan on the back. "We'll see you next week."

Other people began approaching them. Nathan seemed to be friends with the entire church. Kat spotted a sign that said restrooms, and she excused herself and retreated to one until she thought more people would be gone. When she finally walked out, Nathan was talking to a very attractive woman around their age. She had blonde hair and blue eyes that were fixed on his. They looked like a perfect match for one another, like Barbie and Ken. She felt a slight twinge of jealousy but brushed it off. She was only here to get back together with Justin.

Nathan glanced up and saw her. He motioned for her to join them. As she approached, the woman's demeanor changed. She gave her a look that was very familiar—a look Kat was sure she had when she thought about Mandy. This girl had feelings for Nathan. Did he feel the same way about her? Had he given up his chance at love to help Kat?

"Bridgette, this is Katarina. Katarina, Bridgette."

"It's nice to meet you," said Bridgette.

"You as well."

There was an awkward silence.

"Well, I will see you on Wednesday at Bible study," said Bridgette. She and Nathan exchanged a smile, and she left.

"I'm sorry for interrupting your conversation. I wanted to thank you for talking to that couple about me."

"No problem. I told you I could get you a better job and home. I'm still not sure about the Justin thing, but I guess we'll see."

"Two out of four isn't bad," she said jokingly.

He laughed. "Text me tomorrow and tell me when you start. I'll help you move in when you're ready."

"Oh, thank you, but I won't need any help. I can fit everything I have in my car." She studied him for a second.

"What is it?"

"Those people seem to be your friends. You barely know me, yet you're putting your reputation on the line for me, a loser you met less than a week ago. I can't figure out why."

He took her hands and looked into her eyes. Her pulse quickened. "You are not a loser. I have faith in you, Katarina."

Something fluttered in her stomach when he said her name. She pulled her hands out of his. "Well, thank you. I promise not to let you down. I may be many things, but I am not a liar."

"I'm not worried about it. Do you have plans on Wednesday evening? Would you like to come to Bible study?"

Her lip curved to the side. "Sorry, I can't make it. I have to work at the Pancake House."

"Well, if something changes, it starts at seven. You're always welcome to come. If not, then I'll see you next Sunday. I can't wait to meet Chloe."

Kat smiled. "See you next Sunday."

Chapter Seven

Tears streamed down Kat's face as she walked out of the church doors after counseling. As she walked closer to her car, she saw someone standing beside it. It was dark outside, but she would recognize that tall, muscular silhouette anywhere. His warm smile lightened the darkness inside her.

"What are you doing here?" she asked. "I thought I wouldn't see you until Sunday."

He shrugged. "I knew tonight would be hard for you. I didn't want you to be alone."

She looked the same way she did the night he found her. Swollen eyes with mascara streaks trailing down her cheeks. She didn't say anything. She stood there looking at him. She looked so...so broken. Without hesitation, he wrapped his arms around her, and she began to cry. He held her tightly. His heart hurt for her. He knew these emotions weren't only for what she had gone through over the past few weeks but over a lifetime.

His embrace filled her with security.

Kat wanted to stop crying, but the tears kept coming. Tonight was the first time in years, maybe ever, that she had spoken of her past in detail and what it was like growing up with an alcoholic single mother. Memories she had tucked away in the darkest part of her heart, never to remember again, were forced to be recognized and re-lived. She realized that the little girl who had always felt alone and rejected had never left. They had only scratched the surface, and Kat already dreaded next week. They hadn't even gotten to the part where she was taken into state custody.

Dimly, she became aware of a very unfamiliar feeling. A feeling she had never felt before with her mom, Justin, or anyone. What was it? With her head buried in Nathan's chest and his strong arms around her, she figured it out. She felt like she belonged. That Nathan genuinely cared about her and not because he wanted anything from her.

Terrified by her feelings, she quickly pulled away from him.

"Are you okay?"

"Yeah, I just... I feel overwhelmed."

"Sometimes we have to make a bigger mess before we can clean up and get organized."

"I have so much trash in my closet that I'm pretty much buried in it."

"That's why we get rid of the trash and only hold on to what matters."

"I'm doubtful there's anything left of much value when the trash is gone."

"If you put on a pair of dirty glasses, your vision would be blurred and distorted. It wouldn't be the true picture of everything you looked at, but it would affect everything you see. But if you took those dirty glasses off, your vision would be clear and you could see how things truly are. Right now, you are looking at yourself and life through dirty lenses."

She nodded and wiped her face with her hands. "I shouldn't be crying. I got the job today and a new place to live. I start next Monday, and I get to move in tomorrow. I'm very excited. Chloe will be beyond happy, especially if I can get Christmas decorations before her next visit. I have to thank you for all of it. I asked them why they hired me when I don't have the credentials and they don't know me. They said that they would hire anyone that you recommended."

He smiled. "I'm thankful to hear that you now have a better place to live and bring your daughter to stay. That's a couple things off the list. Only a couple more to go."

She studied him for a moment. "Why would you do all of this for me? You barely know me."

"I'm a Christian. I'm only doing what I feel God wants me to do. That's the way I live my life."

"I've never met anyone like you, Nathan Spencer. Even among people who call themselves Christians."

"Well, I'm hopeful that if you keep coming to church with me, that will change."

Kat was doubtful, but she appreciated the sentiment. She reached for her car door.

"Do you mind if I come by and meet Chloe on Saturday? I want to meet her before church on Sunday so that she sees a familiar face."

Kat smiled. "I would like that."

Nathan closed the door for her after she got in, and she waved and drove off. She couldn't help glancing at him in her rearview mirror and mentally revisiting the comfort-filled hug they'd shared.

As Kat drove into her old subdivision, dread made her gut churn. She hated feeling like an intruder whenever she picked up her daughter. She couldn't bear seeing Mandy sporting her new diamond ring—the one she should have been given years ago. She hoped Justin wouldn't be home yet. Her heart might crumble at the sight of him kissing Mandy the way he'd once kissed her.

She pulled into the driveway. She was thankful to see Justin's car wasn't there. Before she could open her car door, Chloe ran toward her with a huge smile. "Mommy!"

Kat held her tight, trying to soak in the lost time. She had missed her so much. She desperately wished they never had to be apart. "Go and get your things, sweetheart. I have a surprise for you."

"What is it?"

"You'll have to wait and find out."

Chloe ran ahead of her into the house, and Kat slowly walked through the door she had left open and stood in her usual spot inside the doorway.

Mandy walked out with her perfectly groomed hair, clothes, and nails, all paid for with Justin's money. "Hi, Kat. Can you please have Chloe home by five-thirty on Sunday? We're taking her to the Christmas light show on Broad Street."

Kat nodded. She noticed Mandy had a bruise under her eye. Had Justin hit her? In their six-year relationship, he had hit her a few times. It happened almost every time he got drunk. Thankfully, it wasn't very often. "What happened to your eye?"

She touched it. "Oh, I ran into the door."

"Mm. That's happened to me before, too."

Mandy quickly looked away and walked back into the kitchen. A moment later, Chloe came out with her things.

They walked out to Kat's car as Justin pulled into the driveway. Kat tried to ignore the way her stomach flipped at the sight of him.

Justin got out of his car and picked Chloe up. "I'm going to miss you, kiddo."

"I will miss you too, Daddy, but it's Mommy's turn. You get me all the time."

"You're right. I can't be selfish." He looked over at Kat. "Have her here by five-thirty on Sunday—"

"I know. Mandy already told me." Kat opened Chloe's door and refused to glance back in Justin's direction. It hurt too much to see him and for him not to want her anymore.

"What's the surprise, Mommy?"

"You will see very soon."

"But I can't wait. I'm too excited! Did you get a TV?"

"You need to be patient."

"Are we going to be walking a lot this time?"

"We don't have to. I have plenty of gas in my car. But we still can, if you want."

"I wouldn't mind walking a little, but not as much as last time."

Kat laughed.

"Do you have Christmas decorations up yet, Mommy?"

"Not yet. I'm hoping by the next time you come."

Chloe sighed. "The next time I come will be on Christmas Day. Daddy said I will spend Christmas morning with him and Mandy and then go to your house after lunch."

Kat rolled her eyes. Why did he get the house and her daughter and then get to set the times when she got to see her? As soon as she could save up some money, she would get a lawyer.

As they pulled into the apartment complex, Chloe asked, "Where are we, Mommy?"

"This is the surprise. I have a new job and apartment."

Chloe's face lit up with sheer joy. "Yay! I hated the old one. I felt a little scared when I was there." They got out of the car, and Kat walked her around the building. "There's a pool!"

"Yes, so you can go swimming when it warms up this summer."

Chloe jumped up and down. "It's so nice, Mommy! How did you get the money to live here?"

"Living here comes with the job."

When they walked into Kat's new apartment, Chloe looked over every square inch with excitement. "It has real carpet! A nice couch! I have my own bed! We don't have to sleep on the couch together!"

Kat watched her explore with tears in her eyes. It made her happy to see that Chloe was so happy for her.

"How did you get such a good job that would give you all of this?"

"Well, I met a nice man. His name is Nathan. He's going to come by tomorrow to meet you. He's been helping me. The furniture and stuff aren't mine. I'm only using it while I live here."

Chloe opened the refrigerator door. There wasn't much food in it, but more than the other one. "This man must love you, Mommy!"

"No, he's just a really nice man."

"Well, I can't wait to meet him and tell him thank you."

The next day, Chloe was coloring at the small kitchen table. Kat was washing dishes, and Christmas music played from Chloe's tablet. A knock sounded, and Kat quickly dried her hands. When she opened the door, she saw a big box and three smaller ones on the ground, and Nathan was holding two giant bags in his arms. He had clearly made a couple of trips before knocking on the door. "What's all this?"

"I wanted to make sure Chloe had Christmas decorations."

Hearing her name, Chloe stopped coloring and ran to the door.

"This is the nice man I was telling you about," Kat told her.

He kneeled to be at eye level with her. "Hi, I'm Nathan. I've heard so many wonderful things about you. Your mother loves you a lot. It's nice to meet you."

Without hesitation, Chloe wrapped her little arms around his neck and hugged him. "Thank you so much for helping my mommy. She's had it hard. My daddy has been very mean and unfair to her. Her old house didn't even have carpet or a bed. We had to sleep together on this dirty old couch she found in someone's trash."

"Chloe!" Kat exclaimed, embarrassed. "Let's invite him inside. We are being rude. It's cold."

Chloe looked at all the stuff. "Is that a Christmas tree?" she asked with excitement.

"It is. Your mother said she didn't have any decorations, so here we are."

Chloe hugged his legs. "You must love my mommy so much."

"I do."

Kat's heart stopped briefly.

"You see, I'm a Christian, Chloe. That means I love everyone, including you and your mom."

"Do you want to marry her?"

Nathan laughed. "It's a different kind of love."

Chloe gave him a puzzled look and then helped bring in the things he had brought.

Once everything was inside and settled, Nathan walked to the door. "Well, it was nice meeting you, Chloe. I should let you ladies get to decorating."

Chloe grabbed his hand. "You can't leave. You should stay and help."

Nathan looked at Kat, with a question in his eyes.

"She's right," Kat said with a smile. "You should stay."

"Okay, let's do this."

Nathan took off his coat and laid it on the couch. They all began pulling decorations from the boxes and bags.

Nathan put the tree together while Kat and Chloe sorted the ornaments.

Chloe held up a princess ornament. "You have good taste in decorations."

Nathan laughed. "I can't take all the credit. I had my friend Bridgette help me. She's an elementary teacher at a nearby school, and I knew she would know more about what a five-year-old girl would like."

Kat lowered her eyes at the mention of her name.

"Well, you both did really good," said Chloe.

"Thank you. I'm glad we met your approval."

They talked and laughed as they decorated the tree. Chloe had barely left Nathan's side since he arrived. It was as if she were drawn to him, and Kat couldn't figure out why. She had a dad who wasn't perfect, but he loved her and was good to her.

"What's this?" asked Kat, giving Nathan a playful smile.

"What?"

"You can't put two reds beside each other. You have to alternate the colors."

"Well, excuse me. Thank you for the ornament lesson. Now that I've been properly schooled, I'll never make that mistake again," he said jokingly as he separated the two ornaments. They shared a laugh.

"Mommy, Nathan, look!" said Chloe as she stood on the coffee table next to them, holding up a picture she had drawn as high as she could.

"Please get down, sweetheart. That's dangerous, and we don't stand on furniture, especially when it's not ours."

"It's mistletoe. You know what you have to do when there's mistletoe."

Kat and Nathan gave each other an awkward glance. "Not this time, sweetheart," said Kat awkwardly.

"Please! You have to."

Kat looked at Nathan. He shrugged, then he looked into her dark arresting eyes and slowly leaned in and kissed her. As soon as his lips touched hers, her body felt weak. She almost dropped the glass ornament in her hand.

A moment later, he pulled back, his gaze swept across her face. "I really should be going. I have an early morning."

Chloe wrapped her arms around his legs. "I don't want you to go."

He kneeled again to be at eye level with her. "I will see you tomorrow at church."

"At church? I've never been before."

"Well, you are going to love it. There are lots of children your age there. They play games and eat snacks. It will be a lot of fun. I will be looking for you."

He stood, and Kat followed him to the door. "I don't know what to say. You did so much. Thank you for everything and for staying.."

"It was fun. Thank you for letting me help."

She sighed in dread. "I guess I'll see you tomorrow."

"You will eventually get used to it and maybe even like it."

She gave him a sarcastic look. "Not likely."

He smiled and then left. Kat closed the door behind him and put her forehead against it. How could she ever repay him for all the nice things he had done for her and now Chloe?

"I like him, Mommy. He's even more handsome than Daddy. I think you should marry him."

Kat laughed. "Get that thought out of your little head right now. That's never going to happen, sweetheart."

"Why not?"

"He would never marry someone like me."

Chapter Eight

Chloe couldn't wait to see Nathan. She talked about him all the way to church. Kat began to worry about how Chloe would react when their arrangement was over. Hopefully she wouldn't mind; it would mean Kat was back with Justin, and they would be a family again.

As they pulled into the very full parking lot, Kat took a deep breath and tried to prepare herself before going in.

Unlike Kat, Chloe was nearly bursting with excitement; after all, Nathan had made church sound like a fun place.

Mike and Linda Murry, Kat's new employers, met them at the doors. "Hello, Kat."

Kat smiled uncomfortably. "This is my daughter, Chloe. Chloe, these are the nice people who gave me the new job and are letting me live in the nice apartment."

Linda reached out to shake Chloe's hand. But the little girl pushed her hand aside and hugged her instead. "Thank you for helping my mommy. She's been working so hard, and her other apartment was so bad. I—"

"We should probably go and find Nathan," Kat interrupted, her face two shades of red.

Linda smiled warmly. "We are looking forward to you starting tomorrow."

"So am I. Thank you again for everything."

"The Lord always provides. We are thankful He can use us," said Mike as he opened the door for them.

Nathan was just inside the doors, and Chloe ran to him as if she had known him all her life. He responded similarly, scooping her up in his arms. "I told you I would be looking for you. Are you ready to see your classroom, make new friends, and meet your teacher? She's very nice. You're going to like her."

"Yes!"

After putting her down, he took her hand, and they started walking down a hallway. Kat followed closely behind. After passing several classrooms, they stopped in a doorway. Kat saw another familiar face: Bridgette. She was Chloe's teacher.

Kat noticed how her face softened the second she saw Nathan. She was clearly in love with him, but like most men, he seemed clueless.

"Hello, Ms. Brigette. Let me introduce you to my good friend Chloe. She will be in your class today."

"Hello, Chloe. We're so happy you're here."

"Hey, I know you. You teach at my school."

Bridgette smiled. "I thought you looked familiar. From now on, you'll have to wave at me when you see me. Would you like to go inside and join the other children? They are playing with play dough."

Chloe nodded. "I like play dough!" She looked back at her mother, who motioned for her to go in. She smiled as she sat by another little girl with pigtails.

Bridgette and Nathan chatted for a moment. Kat didn't join in; she stood and watched Bridgette with a twinge of envy.

Bridgette was innocent and whole—something Kat could never be.

Nathan and Kat sat in the same spot as the week before, and she recognized the man a couple rows in front of them. He had bought her a drink at Allen's the night she almost took her life. She leaned over and whispered in Nathan's ear, "Is that Frank from the bar?"

Nathan looked in the direction she pointed. "It is. I'm so glad he could make it."

"You're good at your job of getting people to come to church. They should give you a raise."

VALERIE ZAHN

He laughed. "I don't work here because of the money. I have an engineering degree."   "You're an engineer? So why are you working here?"

"I feel this is where God wants me to be. For now, anyway. There's a lot more to life than money or success."

Kat shook her head. How could he choose to work at a church instead of the career he had spent so much of his time and money to get? "Have you come to anyone else's rescue like you did for me since you've been working at Allen's?"

"No, and I'm not going to. They fired me. They said I wasn't good for business."

She laughed. "I'm sure that talking to people about Jesus would put a damper on getting wasted."

When the music started, she smiled. She liked this part of the service. As she listened to the lyrics of the second song, tears welled in her eyes. It spoke about God being a loving father to the orphan. If only she had known the love of a father. She had seen glimpses of it in how Justin loved Chloe, how a couple of the foster dads loved their biological children, but not personally. She discreetly wiped her eyes, hoping no one noticed. God may be a loving father for some people, but He had never been one to her. He had never been there for her at all. He had stood by and allowed everyone in her life to use, mistreat, and abuse her.

Kat sat rigid, refusing to let herself feel any emotion for the rest of the song.

Now it was time for the sermon. This was the part she dreaded the most. She wished she could get up and walk out, but Nathan had gone above and beyond to keep his end of their agreement. There was no way she couldn't keep hers.

While the minister spoke, she tuned him out. She planned out her day and week in her mind. She did well at not listening until the end of the sermon. Without wanting to, she heard the pastor say, "I know some of you wonder if God is really good, then why do bad things happen to innocent people? Here's the thing. God never intended for bad things to happen at all. He created a garden where we had everything we would ever need. We were to walk with Him in person and to never feel sadness or hurt. We were never supposed to die. However, when Adam and Eve disobeyed God, sin entered the world and ruined everything. Sin always has consequences, and those consequences never affect only you. They affect your family, friends, and possibly people you will never know. If someone has ever hurt you, that's a consequence of someone's sin. It's not God's fault, but man's. The good news is that God sent Jesus, His only Son, to heal and mend sin's effects. To save and redeem everyone so that the vicious cycle can stop. We do that by asking Jesus into our hearts. It's the only way to experience true joy and happiness. If you've never done this, will you come to the altar and give your heart and life to Jesus?"

A heartbeat of silence passed, and then people slowly got up, walked to the front, and kneeled at the altar one by one. After a few minutes, Frank walked up and joined everyone else. He had tears streaming down his face.

Why is he crying? Kat wondered.

Soon after, Nathan left his seat and kneeled across from Frank. He put his hand on Frank's shoulder and quietly prayed for him.

Kat didn't budge, but no matter what she did, she couldn't get the pastor's words out of her mind.

Chapter Nine

The cold air chilled Kat's bones as she walked out of the church. She pulled her coat in tight. Once again, mascara streaks lined her face and her eyes were swollen. It had been another tough counseling session. She hated remembering her past and the scared, uncertain, and vulnerable little girl she used to be. In many ways, she still was that little girl.

As she walked closer to her car, she saw Nathan standing beside it, waiting for her. She couldn't help but smile. She could use one of his healing hugs after everything she'd just re-lived. "You don't always have to be here when I get out of counseling."

"I won't be. I just know the first couple of visits can be brutal."

"So, it was tough for you, too, when you had counseling?"

"Oh, yeah."

Kat tilted her head, silently asking him to explain.

"You know about me losing my dad at a young age. It was hard when I was little, having my mom take me to the ball field and teach me how to be a man."

"I'm sorry to minimize what you've been through. You seem so normal and put together, whereas I am a completely shattered mess. The thought of being whole seems impossible."

"Well, there's a scripture that says with God, all things are possible."

Kat broke eye contact. She was determined that neither he nor anyone else would ever convert her. God had left her in the dust. She would do the same to Him.

"Do you know what you need, Katarina?"

"A stiff drink?"

"No. A family."

"Well, yeah, that's what we're working for. To get my family back together."

"Yes, but you need an even bigger family, and I want to help you get that, too. Do you have an hour to spare?"

She looked at her phone. Monday nights were the only nights she didn't have to work at the Pancake House. "Yes," she said uncertainly.

Nathan motioned for her to get in his car, and fear pricked her as she obeyed. The last time she'd ridden in here had been the night she almost took her life.

"So where are we going?" she asked Nathan.

"I want you to meet one of the most amazing women on earth. Her name is Ms. Rose. She's all alone with no children. Her only living relative is a sister who lives up north. She hasn't been feeling well for the last couple of weeks, so she hasn't been at church, or I would have already introduced you. She's become like a grandmother to me. My family lives in east Tennessee. It's only a three-hour drive, but my church family is also my family. I'm closer to some of them than my biological family."

They pulled into the driveway of a very small house. They walked up a few stairs onto a little porch, and Nathan knocked on the door. A petite older lady with gray curly hair opened the door. Her eyes lit up when she saw him. "Nathan!" she said as she gave him a big hug. He towered over her as he leaned down, wrapped his broad arms around her, and then released her. "What a gorgeous couple you make. Who is this beautiful young lady?" she asked as she reached out to hug Kat.

"This is my friend Katarina."

Kat gave her an awkward hug, but Ms. Rose didn't seem to care. "Katarina, what a beautiful name for such a beautiful girl." She studied Kat for a second. Compassion was present in her green eyes. She looked at Kat as if she could see into her soul—everything, good and bad, that she had ever done. "Please come in. It's so cold outside."

The small house was warm and cozy, and the scent of cinnamon lingered in the air. Kat looked around the modest living room. It was evident that Ms. Rose didn't have many material things, but what she did have was well kept and tidy.

"I just pulled cinnamon bread out of the oven. Would you like some?"

Nathan got a huge smile. "You know I would."

"What about you, Katarina?"

"I'll take a small piece."

"Please come and have a seat in the kitchen."

They followed her into a small kitchen that was barely big enough for the three of them. A table and four chairs sat crowded in the corner.

Ms. Rose hummed to herself as she cut them each a slice of bread. She seemed thrilled to serve it to them. "What are y'all's plans for Christmas?"

"I'm leaving tomorrow," Nathan said. "I'm going to spend Christmas with my family in east Tennessee."

"What about you, Katarina?"

"I don't have any family besides my daughter. One of my friends invited me to spend Christmas morning with her and her two children, but I would just be in the way. I'll pick up my daughter after lunch and celebrate with her then. For the first time in months, I get to spend an entire week with her. My ex is taking his new girlfriend to

New York City for New Year's. I don't have to take Chloe back until the second of January."

"Since you'll be available for breakfast that morning, would you like to come here? I'll fix something."

"Are you sure? I don't want you to go to any trouble on Christmas."

"It would be no trouble at all. I would love to do it. So, what do you say?"

Kat shrugged. "I guess I'll come. Can I bring something?"

Ms. Rose patted Kat's hand. "Just yourself."

Nathan smiled as he watched them interact, clearly pleased that neither of them would be alone for the holiday.

After they ate the bread, drank a cup of coffee, and chatted for a while, Nathan stood. "I hate to be the bad guy, but I've got to be up early in the morning. I'm volunteering at the community soup kitchen for the homeless."

Ms. Rose brought their coats and walked them to the door. She hugged Nathan and then Kat tightly.

On their drive back to the church and Kat's car, she barely heard anything Nathan said. She was thinking about Ms. Rose. Something drew Kat to her, similar to the way Chloe was drawn to Nathan. Maybe it was because she was alone too? Or perhaps it was that she made Kat feel genuinely cared for. She reminded her of

Ms. Elly. Maybe that was it. Kat hadn't thought about her in ages.

"What's on your mind? You're quiet," said Nathan as he parked the car.

"I was thinking about a nice older lady from my past. Ms. Rose reminds me of her. I haven't thought about her in ages."

"Tell me about her."

Kat smiled. "She lived in the apartment two doors down from ours. When I was scared or felt alone, which was quite often, I visited her. She would always ask me if I had eaten. Usually I hadn't, so she would fix me something to eat—usually a peanut butter and jelly sandwich. Looking back, I realize how much she helped me. She once asked me if I wanted to be like my mom. I, of course, told her no. So she encouraged me to read books, take care of myself, and do everything I could to be different and break the cycle. I thought I had until Justin threw me out. Recently, I've reminded myself of my mother."

"How's that?"

"When Chloe had to come stay with me in my old, rundown apartment. Going to a bar when I was at my darkest point. I realized I'm a broken mess just like she was."

"The difference is, you didn't stay in that rundown apartment. You are getting help, not staying broken. And you are an amazing mother. You are not like your mother at all, Katarina. But perhaps you can find it a little easier to forgive her now that you know how hard life can sometimes be."

"If it hadn't been for you..."

He interrupted her. "It wasn't me. God had me there that night for you. I am as human as anyone. He is the one who makes me different."

She rolled her eyes. "Well, it's getting late. I need to be getting home. Thank you for being here tonight and for introducing me to Ms. Rose. She seems like a nice person."

"She's truly one of the sweetest people I know." Nathan held the car door open for her. Just before she closed it, he said, "Hey, how about you and Chloe spend New Year's with my family and me?"

Kat hesitated. "I'm not a charity case, Nathan. Don't worry about us. We're fine."

"I don't see you as a charity case. You're my friend. As a friend, I'm asking if you'll come."

"You can't just invite us to someone else's house."

"I've already talked to my mom, and she wants you both to come."

"Oh, I would have loved to hear that conversation. 'Hey, mom, can I bring a girl home that I rescued from suicide? She's a complete mess and a loser. She has no family because no one has ever wanted her. Oh, and did

I mention she's bringing the daughter she had out of wedlock?'"

Nathan took a step closer. "Katarina, you are not a loser. You've only been surrounded by losers, and that's why they don't want you. Come on; it would only be for one night. You could come on New Year's Eve and leave after lunch the next day. Please? My mom loves having company and playing hostess."

"Let me ask Chloe. I'll text you and let you know."

"If it's up to Chloe, it's a done deal. I'll text you the address," he said with a joking smile.   She laughed. "She does seem to like you more than me."

He ran his fingers through his hair with a grin, "What's not to like?"

She smiled. He was right. He was flawless. So far, there was nothing about him that even she didn't like. But they had only known each other for a few weeks. He was bound to show his true colors eventually. Right?

Chapter Ten

Kat slowly opened her eyes. Sadness filled her heart. This was the first Christmas morning without Chloe since she was born. She hated that she was missing her running into her room and waking her up. She was missing out on all of her excitement and seeing her glowing smile as she shook and opened each gift. She hated that she wouldn't be in Justin's arms as they watched their daughter enjoy the magic of Christmas. But what she hated most was that Mandy was getting everything she was missing out on. What was Chloe doing right now? Would they keep the tradition of eating cinnamon buns after opening gifts?

Wiping tears from her eyes, she got out of bed. "Feeling sorry for yourself isn't going to change anything, Kat," she said to herself. She walked over to the window and opened the blinds. She wished there was snow, but it didn't often snow in Tennessee around Christmas. It would be more likely in January or February—if it even snowed at all.

"Thank you, God, that I get to see Chloe today. Thank you that I have been able to save a little money to get her a few gifts. Thank you that I now have a good job. Thank you for my new friend, Ms. Rose, and that I don't have to be alone on Christmas morning. Even though I know that I only have to thank you for five things, I also want to thank you for Nathan. Please let him have a wonderful Christmas with His family."

Feeling a little better, she stepped away from the window to get ready to go to Ms. Rose's.

Even though there was no snow, it was still freezing outside. Kat knocked on Ms. Rose's door, which promptly swung open to reveal the smiling woman. Ms. Rose hugged her tightly, as if they were long-lost friends who hadn't seen each other in ages. Kat couldn't remember the last time she had been embraced by anyone other than Chloe and, recently, Nathan.

"Katarina! I'm so glad you made it. Please come inside."

As Kat walked through the door, the savory and sweet aroma grew stronger. Ms. Rose took her coat, and then Kat followed her into the small kitchen. In the middle of the table was the most delicious-looking spread. There were scrambled eggs, bacon, ham, sausage, fried potatoes, biscuits, and gravy. That was only the savory. She also had cinnamon buns cooking in the oven.

"All of this is just for the two of us?"

Ms. Rose laughed at her reaction. "I was hoping you could take some home with you to share with your little girl." Ms. Rose handed her a plate. "Here, get as much as you'd like. Don't be shy."

Kat didn't want to disappoint her, but her thin five-nine frame could only eat so much. Everything looked and smelled delicious.

She waited until Ms. Rose made her plate before she took her first bite. But before Ms. Rose ate, she took Kat's hand and said a prayer. "Thank you, Lord, for this Christmas morning. Let us take time to remember this day and what it truly means. How the world was in despair and darkness, and you brought hope and light by sending your precious son who grew up in a physical body so He could relate to His people in their humanity. Who knows our pain, loneliness, and sorrows because He experienced them too. I love you, Lord. Thank You for my new friend, Katarina. Let her come to know just how much You truly love her and how special she is to You. Amen."

Kat fought back tears. She didn't know why Ms. Rose's prayer affected her, but it did. Trying to get her mind on something else, she took a bite. It was no surprise that the food tasted as wonderful as it looked. "This is amazing. Thank you for inviting me."

"I am so happy you came. I get lonesome a lot, and I love to have people over. When I was younger, my husband and I entertained a great deal; he enjoyed it just as much as I did. I miss that wonderful man, especially today."

Kat stopped eating and put her hand on Ms. Rose's but didn't say anything.

"I can tell you're familiar with loss, too," said Ms. Rose. Kat nodded. "Would you like to talk about it?"

Kat thought about it for a moment. If Ms. Rose knew she had a daughter outside of wedlock, she might not want to befriend her anymore. However, if she was going to reject her, she would rather it be now when they were only beginning to get to know each other. Besides, Kat knew she was many things, but she wasn't a liar and would never hide behind false pretenses. So she told her about her past—even more than she had intended to, even more than she had told Nathan. Ms. Rose never flinched or acted like any of it surprised her or changed her opinion of Kat. Unfortunately, bringing up the past always brought her to tears.

When she was done, Ms. Rose walked around the table and put her arms around Kat's shoulders. "You've been through a great deal in your life, young lady. I know the Lord wants to heal you from the pain of your past, but it will take time. You're going to have to trust Him. Attending church, counseling, and reading your Bible are wonderful first steps. I'm very proud of you for being willing to do it."

"I'm not doing it for the right reasons. Nathan and I have an arrangement, and I have to do those things for him to keep his side of it."

"That's okay. The reason doesn't matter. You are still doing it, and that's something to be proud of."

Kat wasn't sure about that, but it was nice to have someone else who seemed to care about her like Nathan did. She didn't have a single memory of anyone telling her they were proud of her. "I'm sorry I've ruined this wonderful breakfast by blabbing about myself."

"You didn't ruin it. Getting to know you only made it better."

"Enough about me. Tell me about this wonderful man you mentioned earlier."

"My Henry. Oh, he was the most amazing man. He was tall and thin, with dark hair and blue eyes. He was the most handsome man I had ever laid eyes on. He loved God with all his heart, and as an extension of that great love, he loved other people. He made me feel like I mattered more to him than anything in this world. I can't tell you how much I miss being in his arms. However, I know where he is, and because of that, I would never ask him to come back, even if he could. But I long for the day that I'll be with him again." When describing him, it was almost as if she were describing Nathan, and then she said it. "Nathan reminds me of a younger version of him. He's such a wonderful young man. I wish they could have met, but my Henry died a few years before I met Nathan. I pray that whomever Nathan marries will love him and cherish him the way I did my Henry."

Kat looked at her phone and gasped. "I'm so sorry to eat and leave, but I must be going. I've got to pick up my daughter. How about, instead of me taking food with me, Chloe and I come in the morning for breakfast? I would love for her to meet you."

Ms. Rose's face lit up. "Oh, I would love that! I love children." She fetched Kat's coat, then walked her to the door and gave her a big hug. "Be careful and enjoy your precious girl." "Thank you for everything, and Merry Christmas. We will see you tomorrow."

"I look forward to it."

As Kat pulled into her old subdivision, she noticed multiple cars in people's driveways as families gathered to celebrate the holidays. She envied them. All she had ever wanted was a family, and being with Justin had given her one. It was small because she and Justin were both only children and all of his family lived in California, but it was the only one she had ever really belonged to.

She held her breath as she walked to the front door and tried to prepare herself for how hard it would be to see them together as a family.

Justin answered her knock, and the smell of cinnamon buns wafted through the open door. It made her heart ache. How could they have carried on with the tradition that she'd started? It infuriated her to think that Mandy was filling her role.

"Chloe went to get her things," said Justin with little emotion. Kat nodded. "Chloe has mentioned someone named Nathan several times. I don't want my daughter around the men you're dating. I won't have it. You are not to see him when Chloe's around."

Kat burned with anger. Who was he to tell her who and when she could see anyone? He didn't want Chloe to be around people she dated, yet she could live with the woman he was dating? She bit her lip to keep from saying something she might regret. If she made him angry, would he prevent her from taking Chloe home for Christmas and the week?

Thankfully, just as she was about to lose her cool, Chloe ran to her. "Mommy! Merry Christmas!"

"Merry Christmas, sweetheart. Are you ready to go?"

"Yep!"

Kat opened the door while Justin hugged Chloe. "Have her back home on the second by six. She'll have school the next day and will need to get back into her routine." He looked over at Chloe. "Have fun with your mom. I'll miss you, but we'll see you in a few days. I love you." Chloe kissed his cheek. "I love you too, Daddy."

As they got into the car, Kat asked Chloe what she had told her dad about Nathan. "I told him that he was really good to you and that he was really, really handsome—more handsome than him."

Kat laughed. "No wonder he responded like he did."

"Are we going to see Nathan today?"

"Not today. He's spending Christmas with his family. However, he invited us to visit him and his family for New Year's in east Tennessee if you want to go."

"I do! I do!"

"We can go only on one condition."

"What?"

"You can't tell your dad."

She took her fingers and pretended to zip her lips. "It will be our little secret."

"Okay, then I guess we'll go."

"Yay!"

When they walked into Kat's apartment, Chloe took her things to her room. Then she brought out her coloring book and crayons, went to the kitchen table, and started coloring.

"Chloe, don't you want to open your presents?"

"Presents? I didn't think you could get any."

"I kept my second job so I would be able to."

Chloe jumped up and hugged her mother. "I love you so much, Mommy." Kat pointed to the tree, and the little girl's eyes widened. "Are those for me?"

Kat couldn't help but grin as she nodded.

Chloe ran to them. "Wow, Mommy! There are three!"

"Open them."

Chloe opened the first one. "A unicorn!" She squeezed it and then hugged her mother. "I love it!"

"You're not done yet. Open the others."

She opened the second one. "A dolly! I will name her Amy." She opened the third one. "A craft kit!" She ran to Kat and hugged her. "Thank you, thank you, thank you!"

"You are very welcome, sweetheart. I wish I could have given you more, but at least I could get you something."

"This was plenty. I love all of them." Chloe ran to her bedroom and came back out, holding something behind her back. "Close your eyes."

Kat did as she asked, and Chloe put something in her hands.

"I made this for you at school."

"A star! It's just what I wanted. Thank you. I love it!" Kat hugged her.

The following day, Kat and Chloe went to see Ms. Rose.

Chloe was asking all sorts of questions on the way.

"You are going to love her," Kat said. "She is a very nice lady. Nathan introduced me to her."

"Well, in that case, I will definitely like her."

Kat laughed. "Why do you like Nathan so much?"

"He's so nice, fun, and funny. Don't you like him, Mommy?"

"I do. I don't know if I like him as much as you do, though."

"Well, you should. Look at all that he's done for you."

Kat parked the car, and Chloe took her hand as they walked to the door. Chloe rang the doorbell, and Ms. Rose opened it with her usual warm and joyful smile.

"Katarina!" she said as she hugged her. "And who is this beautiful girl?"

"This is my daughter Chloe."

Chloe studied Ms. Rose for a minute, then hugged her.

"You are as lovely as your mother. Please come in."

"It smells so good," said Chloe, looking around the small house. They all sat down at the table, and Ms. Rose handed them a plate. Kat remembered not to take a bite until after the prayer this time.

As Ms. Rose and Kat bowed their heads, Chloe gave them a strange look. She almost took a bite, but Kat stopped her. She whispered in Chloe's ear, "She's going to pray over the food before we eat."

Chloe shrugged. Prayer wasn't something she was familiar with. She watched her mom and Ms. Rose close their eyes while Ms. Rose talked to God. Another thing that was foreign to her. Kat put her arm on Chloe's back when she got antsy during the lengthy prayer.

As they ate, Kat and Chloe went on and on about how wonderful the food was. They visited and had such a good time. Ms. Rose loved Chloe. She treated her like she was her very own granddaughter. Chloe loved her attention and her doting. The fact that she gave her a bag of candy as they were leaving only sealed their bond.

"Are you free on Wednesday evening after the holidays?" asked Ms. Rose.

Since Kat had quit her job at the Pancake House last week, she now had her evenings free. "Yes, I'm free."

"Would you like to come to my Bible study group at the church? It only lasts an hour."   Everything in her wanted to say no. "Sure. I'll come."

"Wonderful! I look forward to seeing you there."

"I want to go too, Mommy."

"I have to take you home on Sunday, sweetheart. You will be with your dad then."

Chloe's shoulders sagged.

Kat sighed when she got into the car. What had she gotten herself into? She had been keeping her end of the bargain and read a section from the Bible each night. Well, she mostly skimmed over it, but her eyes looked at every word.

She sighed again. Maybe she would go at least once and then come up with an excuse not to have to go back.

Chapter Eleven

Kat and Chloe were an hour and a half into their three-hour drive to Johnson City to see Nathan and meet his family. Chole was getting a little antsy. Kat looked at the clock. She wanted to ensure they were there by six because Nathan wanted them to be there in time for dinner. Their New Year's Eve tradition was to eat finger foods and play games until midnight.

Kat stopped at a rest stop for her and Chloe to stretch their legs and go to the restroom. She opened Chloe's door and helped her out. "We have ten minutes before we need to be back on our way. Are you ready? Let's go!"

They briskly walked toward the building, making it a game. They played a game of tag on their way to the car and were soon back on the road.

The closer they got, the more nervous Kat became.

Why are we going? These people are strangers. It's not like I've even known Nathan for that long. What if Justin finds out and keeps me from seeing Chloe?

She contemplated turning around and returning home, but Nathan would be disappointed, and Chloe would never forgive her. Chloe had been through so much over the last several months, and she absolutely loved Nathan. She was willing to be uncomfortable for less than twenty-four hours for something that would make Chloe happy.

They turned into the driveway of a large house on the lake. She was nearly shaking from nervousness. She just sat in the car, not wanting to go inside. Memories returned of being made fun of in school by the rich kids. She felt like that little girl in elementary school, wearing clothes from Goodwill and a snack from the local food bank. She wanted to run and hide like she used to.

"Let's go, Mommy!"

Kat blinked hard and slowly got out of the car. She could smell the food even from outside. She opened the trunk and grabbed a small bag with their things. "It's less than twenty-four hours," she whispered to herself again, trying to work up the courage to walk toward the door.

Then the front door opened, and Nathan walked out with a huge smile.

"Nathan!" Chloe ran to him, and he picked her up. "Your house is so big! Are you rich?" Nathan laughed.

"This isn't my house. It's my parents' house. Do you want to go inside and meet them? They can't wait to meet you and your mom."

Chloe nodded with excitement.

Nathan's family stood in the entryway to greet them. "Everyone, meet my friends Katarina and Chloe."

Nathan's mom reached out and hugged her and then Chloe. Why were all the people associated with Nathan so huggy?

"This is my mom, Donna." Kat smiled in greeting. A gray-haired man a little shorter than Nathan reached out his hand, and Kat shook it. "This is my stepdad, Kevin." A teenage boy who looked like a younger version of Nathan and an attractive girl who looked to be around twelve stood next to their parents with inviting smiles. "And this is my younger brother Josh and my little sister Beth."

"It's nice to meet you all," Kat said. "Thank you for inviting us."

Chloe clung to Nathan. She needed a little time to warm up to everyone.

Donna motioned for Kat to follow her. "Come with me. I'll show you where you and Chloe will be sleeping."

Kat followed her down a hallway. The walls were covered with family photos. Envy gripped her heart. Did they realize how lucky they were? "Your home is beautiful, Ms. Spen..." She caught herself. She remembered her last name had changed after she had remarried.

"You can call me Donna. Thank you. The Lord has blessed us. We are so glad you could come. I've heard a lot of wonderful things about you and Chloe." She walked her into a large bedroom, grand and nicely decorated like the rest of the house. "Please make yourself comfortable."

Kat set the bag down while Donna stood in the doorway, staring at her. Kat gave her an embarrassed smile. "You have nothing to worry about, Donna. I know I'm not the type of woman you want your son to bring home. Nathan deserves someone much better than me. We are only friends."

"I'm sorry, sweetheart. You misread me. You remind me of myself. I was once a single mom trying to survive a dark time when all hope seemed gone too."

Tears welled up in Kat's eyes. "Do you have any advice?"

"The best advice I could give is to cling to God and don't give up. Things will get better. In terms of my son, I'm very proud of him for helping you through this season of your life. Regarding whom he dates and marries, that's between God, him, and the girl he chooses. Please know that in this family, there is no judgment."

Kat wiped a tear from the corner of her eye. "Thank you."

"Take a minute for yourself. When you're ready, come out and get some food. We have all sorts of things to choose from. I tend to get carried away on the holidays. After we get a bite, we'll play some games. We will eat and play until midnight."

"It sounds fun," said Kat.

Donna smiled and closed the door behind her.

Nathan and Chloe sat on the floor in the living room. Nathan was shuffling a stack of Uno cards when Chloe put her little hand on his shoulder.

"Thank you for making my mommy so happy," she said. "She's been sad for a long time. My daddy has been very mean to her. Even when she looks at me sometimes, I see the sadness in her eyes. But with you, she is always happy."

"If I have anything to do with it, Chloe, I will make sure that happiness never fades."

When Kat walked out, she saw Chloe playing a game with Nathan. Kat marveled at how good he was with Chole. He was going to be an amazing father one day. Whomever he married would be a lucky woman.

"Hey, Mommy, I've already beaten Nathan twice."

Kat smiled. "Remember, you can't always win. Right, Nathan?"

Nathan laughed, "Yeah. You are so good at this game, but sometimes others need to win too." Nathan studied Kat for a second. She was so beautiful. Her light blue sweater complimented her slick dark hair and deep brown eyes. "Are you okay?"

"I'm fine," said Kat.

"Are you ready to get some food?"

"If you are."

"Come on, kiddo. Let's get something to eat."

"My daddy calls me kiddo, too."

Nathan and Kat swapped a glance. "Oh, I'm sorry. Is there another name you want me to call you?"

"You can call me your Chloe girl."

Nathan looked at Kat for her approval. Kat shrugged. "Okay, Chloe girl, would you like some macaroni and cheese? My mom made it especially for you because she knew you would like it."

"Yes! Thank you!" Nathan reached out his hand, and Chloe took it. Kat loved seeing their sweet bond and interactions, but it also concerned her. What would happen if Justin entered her life again?

After dinner, the family played games. While playing a game of spoons, Kat looked around the table at all the smiling faces. She tried to bask in that moment of being a part of a family. She wished time would stop so she could soak it in.

After spoons, the family went to the basement and over to the dartboard. Kat didn't want to brag, but she was actually good at this one. Being raised by a mom whose second home was the bar, dartboards had been very accessible, and she'd had plenty of time to practice.

After she hit the bull's eye three times, Nathan was clearly impressed. Everyone cheered her on. Even though she was slaughtering him, she kept catching him staring with a huge grin on his face. He laughed and joked with her, and she couldn't help but notice the way his hand brushed her lower back as he passed to retrieve their darts.

He couldn't help but be taken by her smile. Since they had met, he had never seen her smile as much as she had that night, and he hadn't realized how funny she was. Her physical beauty was undeniable, but she was just as beautiful on the inside; it was only covered by a thick shell put in place for protection.

As everyone sat down for the next game, Kat decided to sit it out. She walked out onto the balcony overlooking the lake. She admired the serene beauty of the moon's reflection on the water. After a few minutes, Nathan came out to join her. "This view never gets old. I would love to live on the water someday. What about you?"

"Right now, I'm just trying to survive the present. I try not to think about the future too much. Nothing has turned out the way I wanted it to, so why disappoint myself by thinking ahead?"

"Are you having fun?"

Kat nodded. "You're very lucky. Your family is wonderful. Being here makes me feel torn. Part of me wants to jump right in and be in the mix of it all, but another part wants to guard myself for fear of being rejected again." Nathan stepped closer to her while she continued, "It does a number on your self-esteem when the one person in the world who knows you better than anyone, the person you love the most, stops loving you and wants someone else."

Her eyes met Nathan's, and the look in his eyes shifted. It went from sympathetic to empathetic. "He's an idiot."

"Nathan Spencer, the pastor. Did something unkind actually come out of your mouth?"

He looked deep into her eyes. "I don't regret what I said. It's the truth."

The way he looked at her made her pulse race. The intense look on his face left her speechless. She felt a rush of relief when the sliding glass door opened, and Chloe walked out. "Come on, Nathan! We are going to play Uno. I want to beat you again."

Kat and Nathan laughed. Nathan took Chloe's hand and walked inside with her.

Soon after the game of Uno was finished, Chloe fell asleep on the couch. Nathan picked her up and carried her to the room she and Kat were staying in.

When he came out, Donna looked at the clock. "It's eleven fifty-nine."

The family formed a circle, and Kat followed their lead. As soon as it turned midnight, the family took the hand of the person next to them. Kate tried to put out of her mind how her hand fit perfectly in Nathan's.

Nathan's stepdad Kevin began to pray. "Heavenly Father, we thank you for the year that just passed. Thank you for our health, blessings, and Your amazing provision. We thank You most for Jesus, who is and will always be our only hope, and the gift of Your Holy Spirit that dwells within us. As we go into this new year, let us be salt and light to our neighbors. Let us live in such a way that people see You in us. Please use us for Your honor and glory. Please keep us safe and healthy as we walk in obedience to You and Your will. I thank You for my family and our new friends Katarina and Chloe. I pray Your love will surround them, and they will come to comprehend how wonderful You truly are. In Jesus' name, we pray."

In unison, everyone but Kat said, "Amen."

Kevin leaned over and kissed his wife.

Nathan gave Kat a side hug. "Happy New Year, Katarina. I'm thankful God put you in my path."

Chapter Twelve

As Kat walked into the church, her heart beat so hard it felt like it would burst inside her chest. She never in a million years would have thought she, of all people, would attend a Bible study. Signs in the foyer pointed in the direction of the classroom. The door of the adjacent classroom was open too, and she saw Nathan inside. He smiled and waved to her, and she waved back. It had only been three days since she'd seen him last, but it seemed like it had been much longer.

As always, Ms. Rose greeted her at the door with a warm smile followed by a hug. "I'm so glad you made it. Come in. I'll introduce you to some very nice ladies."

Chairs were arranged in a circle around the room, and Kat's heart beat even faster when she saw the twelve or so other women occupying them. The only one she recognized other than Ms. Rose was Bridgette, who probably wasn't thrilled to see her there. Knowing how she felt about Mandy, Kat didn't blame her.

Ms. Rose put her arm around Kat and got everyone's attention. "I would like to introduce you to my dear friend Katarina."

Kat's hands were sweaty. She wanted to run out of the room, drive home, and never return. But instead, she stood there feeling awkward and smiled as the other women smiled back at her.

Bridgette approached her. "I'm glad you could come. I'm sure Nathan is happy you're here too."

Kat lifted a shoulder. "I'm not sure if he even knew I was coming."

"Aren't you guys dating?"

"No... I mean, yes." She sighed. "It's complicated."

"Nathan is an amazing man. The best man I know. Whatever you do, please don't hurt him. He's been through a lot."

"Yeah, I know it was hard on him losing his dad so abruptly and at such a young age."

"I wasn't referring to that. But yes, that was hard too, I'm sure."

"What were you referring to? Did someone hurt him?"

"He hasn't told you?"

Kat shook her head.

Bridgette bit her lip, clearly torn. But she said, "He was engaged a couple years ago to a girl named Nicole. She's the pastor's daughter. Nathan caught her and his best friend kissing one night after a meal here at the church. He broke things off, and she married his best friend a few months later. He ended up losing his fiancée and best friend at the same time. They had purchased a house together—the house Nathan lives in now. It's taken him a while to heal from it. You're the first girl he's dated since it happened. I really care about him and don't want him ever to get hurt like that again."

Kat's eyes filled with tears. She had no idea he had been hurt like that. Her heart ached for him. She remembered the look of empathy on his face when she'd expressed the pain of being cheated on. He knew what that felt like. She wouldn't wish that feeling on anyone, especially Nathan. How could someone cheat on such a wonderful man? It was clear that Brigette cared about him. "Thank you for telling me," she said to Bridgette. "I didn't know. He's been helping me sort out the problems in my life; he never mentioned that he had some too. You have nothing to worry about. I care about him very much and I would never hurt him intentionally. I'm far from perfect, but I'm not a cheater."

As soon as the words left her mouth, she realized she *was* a cheater. It felt like she had been punched in the stomach. She had cheated with Justin while he was still

107

married. All these years, she had never considered the pain she had caused his ex-wife. She loathed Mandy, yet she was no better or different than her.

Ms. Rose called for the group to sit down. How was she supposed to focus when all she could think about was what she had done? If Nathan knew, he would want nothing to do with her. And that would be exactly what she deserved.

Ms. Rose leaned over to Kat. "Are you okay, sweetheart? You look pale."

"I'm fine. I'm just uncomfortable being here."

"You are in good company. You won't be called out or called on." Ms. Rose quieted the ladies and got their attention. "Let's open our Bible to Matthew, chapter one. We will briefly look at verses one through six, which is Jesus' lineage. Most mentions of lineage are focused on the men, but this account mentions some of the women. So we will look at a few of these women and ask ourselves why they are there. First is Tamar. Tamar was wronged by her father-in-law Judah. In their culture, the brother next in line was obligated to marry his brother's widow to give him an heir. After his first and second sons died after being married to her, Judah thought she had killed them. However, it was their wickedness that had caused it. He didn't keep his word to have his third son marry Tamar, so she took matters into her own hands and tricked Judah by dressing up like a prostitute. Judah slept with her, and she became pregnant. Her story consists of trickery, yet she is in the lineage of Jesus.

"Let's look at another woman mentioned, Rahab. Rahab was a prostitute. She knew of God's great power and rescued two of the Israelite spies because of it. They told her that when their people came and made war against her people, she was to tie a crimson cloth from her window. She did, and she and her family were spared. Now she is in the lineage of Jesus and known for her faith.

"Another lady was Ruth. I will make her story brief. If you haven't read it, read the book of Ruth. It's a beautiful story. She was a pagan woman who worshipped pagan gods. Out of love for her mother-in-law, she converted, and now she's here in the lineage of Jesus.

"Now, the last woman we will look at is Bathsheba. The Bible says nothing negative about her at all. She was, in many ways, a victim. King David was on his rooftop and saw her bathing. Even though she was married, he called for her and had sex with her. He killed her husband to cover up the pregnancy, and he married her. She is also in the lineage of Jesus.

"We have looked at four imperfect women with very imperfect backgrounds. All of them are in the lineage of Jesus, and some of the men in Jesus's line are just as flawed. I hope this gives much hope for you and me today. No matter our families, backgrounds, or pasts, we are all welcomed into God's family. Would anyone like to add to what I just went over?"

One woman raised her hand and spoke, but Kat didn't hear a word she said or what the group discussed. She could hardly believe the Bible had stories about prostitutes and adultery and that these people made up Jesus' lineage.

The sick feeling in Kat's gut returned as class wrapped up. She desperately didn't want to lose Nathan as a friend.

Ms. Rose hugged her before she walked out the door. "I'm so glad you came. Did you enjoy it?"

"I actually did."

"I hope you'll come back next week."

Kat smiled but didn't commit. As she was leaving, she heard her name.

"Katarina!" Recognizing his deep voice, she pretended she didn't hear him and kept walking toward the door.

He called out again, and then footsteps pounded toward her. Not wanting to face him, she slowly turned around without making eye contact. "How did it go?"

"It was good. Hey, I really need to be going. I'll see you on Sunday." She pivoted and nearly ran to her car.

Nathan watched her go. Why was she avoiding him? Everything had seemed fine when she and Chloe left after lunch on New Year's Day. Had someone at church offended her? Or perhaps something had gone wrong with Justin.

Whatever it was, Nathan was determined to find out.

Chapter Thirteen

Kat rolled onto her back for what seemed like the tenth time and stared at the ceiling. All she could think about was Nathan and what she'd learned. How could anyone be so foolish to want another man more than him? She also couldn't shake the feeling that he may never want to speak to or have anything to do with her once he knew she had cheated with someone.

Until now, she hadn't realized how much she cared for Nathan. She tried to convince herself it was only as a friend, but there was something more. She loved the security she felt in his embrace and how his mere presence put her at ease. Sometimes the way he looked at her gave her butterflies, and even though she acted like it bothered her, she loved it when he called her by her full name. She sighed,

"He's way too good for you. He deserves someone like Bridgette. Besides, you still love Justin.

She rolled back onto her side and glanced at the clock. Only half an hour had passed since she'd last looked at it. She had to get up in three hours to get ready for work. Trying hard to think about something—anything—else, she settled on the lesson from Bible study. About the imperfect women who were in the lineage of Jesus. She had spent her life thinking she was a lost cause, but maybe there was hope for her. Perhaps God could one day love her.

At some point, she must have fallen asleep, because she jolted awake at the sound of her alarm. She groaned and rolled out of bed to get ready for work, stopping at the bedroom window with her eyes half-cracked.

"Thank you, God, for Chloe. Thank you for my good friend, Elaina, whom I need to reach out to because it's been way too long. Thank you for my friendship with Nathan, even though I'm sure it will be over soon. Thank you for a nice place to live and that I only have a few minutes' walk to work. Amen."

As Kat showed an apartment to a lovely couple, she got a text from Nathan. He asked if she'd like to get coffee later. She didn't respond because she didn't know what to say. She had to tell him about what she'd done in her past, but she wasn't ready. Maybe she would put it off until next week. She owed it to Chloe to let her see him one last time before he wanted nothing to do with them anymore.

Kat was intentionally late for church that morning. She got there just as the band was starting to play.

Nathan leaned over when she slid into the seat next to him. "I didn't think you were coming."

She smiled awkwardly but didn't give him an explanation.

"Is everything okay with you? You've seemed a little strange since you left my parents' house on New Year's."

"Everything is fine."

Kat barely heard a word of the sermon. She needed a plan. How could she leave after it was over without engaging in conversation?

She knew she was acting strange, and that Nathan had noticed. She had never been a liar, mostly because she always spoke her mind despite the consequences. It seemed to get her in as much trouble as it would have if she had just lied.

After the final prayer, Kat quickly stood with her purse and keys in hand.

"Ms. Rose wanted me to invite you over for lunch today," Nathan said, giving her a strange look. "I'm going. I thought we could catch up. We haven't talked in a few days."

She bit her lip. "Ah, I can't today. I'm... I'm really busy with... with things. I really should be going. Please tell Ms. Rose I said hello. We'll do it another time."

Bridgette chose the perfect moment to approach Nathan, and Kat took the opportunity to dart toward the door.

Kat walked into her apartment after a nice long jog. When she was in high school, she had been on the track team. Running helped her deal with her anxiety and worry. She had run countless miles with the kind of life she had lived. Her trim, toned figure reflected it.

A knock sounded at the door as she was getting ready to take a shower, and she paused to peek through the peephole.

It was Nathan.

Her heart sank to her stomach, and her flushed cheeks turned an even darker red. "I'll be right there," she hollered, running to the bathroom to turn off the water. She walked back into the living room and opened the door, trying to look unruffled. "Please come in. I'm sorry for my appearance; I just got back from a run."

"No worries. It's a good look on you."

There was an awkward silence for a moment. Kat found it difficult to make eye contact with him. "Can I get you something to drink?"

"No, I'm good. I won't be staying long. I'm here because I have to know. Have I done or said something to offend you?"

"Not at all."

"Then what's going on? Please don't lie to me. I want the truth."

Kat sighed and motioned to her sofa. "Please have a seat." Her heart pounded against her ribcage as he sat. "Are you sure I can't get you something to drink?"

"No, I don't want anything. I only want you to tell me what's going on."

Kat paced back and forth, wringing her hands. "I don't know where to start. After I tell you this, you may not want to be friends anymore."

"Start anywhere. Just tell me something."

She took a deep breath. "When I met Justin, I knew he was married, and I dated him anyway. He told me they were separated, but he was still married, and we had a child together. So even though I have never cheated on anyone personally and never would, I'm still just as guilty because I took part in it."

Nathan looked at her as if expecting to hear more. When she said nothing else, he asked, "Is that it?"

"Well, yes," she said with tears in her eyes.

He stood and took her hands in his. He brushed her hair out of her face. "I get it, Katarina. You have a past. You've never tried to hide it from me. And it's just that—the past. Let's leave it there. What does this have to do with you and me and our friendship?"

She stepped away from him and began to pace again. "At the Bible study this past Wednesday, Bridgette told me that you've been cheated on and asked me not to hurt you. She deeply cares about you, and I just figured that when you knew about my past, you would want nothing to do with me anymore."

He sighed. "I wish she hadn't told you. That wasn't her place."

"Yeah, well, I wish you had been the one to tell me. I've spilled my guts out to you, and you rarely tell me anything about yourself."

"I came close to telling you when we were out on the balcony at my parent's house the other night, but you were hurting, and I didn't want to make it about me. I wanted to be there for you."

"Well, did you ever think I want to be there for you, too? We're friends. It's not one-sided. I want to know what you've been through and what's bothering you. I want to know when you are hurting and what triggers you."

He gazed into her eyes, and her chest rose and fell as her pulse quickened.

He took a step back. "Thank you for expressing your feelings to me and for being honest," he said. "You're a good friend. I'm sorry I haven't been as open with you as you have been with me. I will try to do better." He walked to the door. "I won't take up any more of your evening. Next time, please don't act weird. Just tell me what's bothering you."

She smiled and nodded.

His gaze stayed on her for a long moment and then left.

Chapter Fourteen

Kat knocked and waited. Finally, after a few minutes, Nathan opened the door. A rush of heat ran through her when she saw his bare chest and a chiseled six-pack.

"Sorry," he said as he reached for a shirt and quickly put it on. "What are you doing here?"

She didn't say anything, fearing she would sound like Elmer Fudd when the words came out. She lifted a few plastic bags and ducked under his arm.

"You can't be here. I don't want you or Chloe to get the flu."

"I'm wearing a mask. I'll wash my hands."

"Please, Katarina."

"I'm going to stay with you for a little while. I want to make sure you're set before I leave."

He sighed, clearly not inclined to argue with her. "I'm sorry for the mess," he said as he disappeared through an open door—probably his bedroom to lay down.

"This is nothing. I'm used to picking up after Justin."

Kat looked around his house. To her surprise, it was relatively tidy for a bachelor and nicely decorated. His ex-fiancée had probably helped him with that before she cheated on him.

Kat unloaded the bags she'd brought. When she took out the thermometer, she washed it in the sink and walked into the room he had entered. It was a simple bedroom, with a pull-up bar above the door and weights in the corner on the other side of his bed. That explained the chiseled abs she kept trying to get out of her head.

She walked closer to his bed. "Here, put this under your tongue."

He opened his mouth, and she placed it in. Within seconds, it began beeping and flashing red, indicating fever.

"Have you taken any medicine?"

"Not yet. I haven't got around to it."

She went back to the kitchen and pulled out a bottle of Ibuprofen from one of the bags, then opened his refrigerator and grabbed a bottle of water. She returned to his room and gave him a couple pills to take. Then she put a cool cloth on his forehead to bring down his temperature.

"Have you eaten anything?"

He shook his head no.

"Nathan Spencer!" She warmed up a can of chicken noodle soup and brought it to him.

"How did you know I was sick?" he asked after he was done eating. He already sounded a little better.

"Ms. Rose called and told me. She was worried about you. She said you sounded awful when you called and told her you wouldn't be at Bible study tonight."

"I hope you don't catch this. It's terrible. But I am really glad you came. I haven't had anyone take care of me since..."

"Nicole? You can talk to me about her. It's not like we are really dating. I haven't held back anything about Justin."

"I don't like talking or thinking about her. It's too painful."

"I can understand that. Did she decorate your house? It looks like it's had a feminine touch."

"Yeah, I bought this house a few months before we were to be married and, well... you know the rest of the story."

"I'm sorry. I bet she regrets every day that she let someone like you get away. If she doesn't, she should."

His gaze sharpened on hers. "You've never been to my house before. It's nice to have you here, and it means a lot that you would come by and make sure I was okay."

"My motives for being here aren't entirely unselfish. Today is Valentine's Day, and I didn't want to be alone."

"A girl like you should never be alone on Valentine's Day. If I wasn't sick, I would have taken you out to dinner."

"And a guy like you deserves to be taken care of when he isn't feeling well."

They looked into each other's eyes, and Kat found it hard to breathe.

She jumped up from the chair beside his bed and picked up the thermometer. "I should retake your temp to make sure it's coming down."

Instead of putting it in his mouth, she handed it to him. Her heart kicked up a notch when his hand touched hers.

They waited in awkward silence for the thermometer to beep.

"Good news. You are going to live." She handed him a bottle of Gatorade and forced him to drink. "You need to stay hydrated to get better."

"I know you didn't have good examples of how to care for someone. How did you learn to do all of this?"

"When I met Justin, I was in college, studying to be a nurse. I ended up getting pregnant and dropping out."

"What made you want to become a nurse?"

"Ask me again some other time. I don't want to get into it now. But in terms of being nurturing, what helped me was a nice lady in one of the foster homes I lived in. She was always very loving and kind to me. I never responded to her affection because I knew my mom would get me back. I guess I was trying to avoid being heartbroken when I had to leave. Anyway, one night, I came down with the flu. I had a terribly high fever. She treated me like I was her own daughter and took the best care of me. She also gave me a new perspective of a mother figure. I knew if I ever became a mom one day, I wanted to be just like her—loving, kind, and present."

"You are an amazing mother, Katarina. Justin should be groveling at your feet to get you back."

She avoided his gaze. "Well, that's never going to happen. He would never stoop to acknowledge that he needs someone. He made me feel like he was the only man who could ever love me."

Nathan took her hand. "Like about so many other things, he lied to you."

His touch filled her with security. "I should probably be going. Can I get you anything before I leave?"

"No, you've got me set."

"Well, don't hesitate to call or text if you need anything. I will come right over."

"Thank you, Katarina. I appreciate everything you've done for me."

"As do I, Nathan. I owe you a lot. More than I could ever repay. You've been good to Chloe and me."

"You owe me nothing. But I hope we can always be friends, regardless of how things turn out between you and Justin."

"I would like that too." They lingered for a moment, lost in each other's eyes. Then Kat said, "Please stay in bed and I'll let myself out."

As Kat was walking out of Nathan's house, Bridgett was walking up to the porch. "How's our patient doing?" she asked.

"A little better. He gets more medicine in two hours. If you're still here, will you make sure he gets it?"

Bridgette nodded.

Kat got into her car, trying to ignore the pang of envy. She couldn't deny that Bridgette, was a better match for him than she could ever be in every way.

Chapter Fifteen

To avoid awkward conversations and feeling uncomfortable, Kat had stopped arriving early for church. She made sure to arrive when the music started. As she walked in, she noticed Nathan wasn't in their usual spot. Her eyes searched the large room for him, but she didn't see him. Then she remembered he was still home recovering from the flu. She turned to leave, but someone caught her by the arm.

It was Ms. Rose with a huge smile. "You can sit with me this morning."

Kat nodded and followed her to her seat.

After the music, everyone sat down, and someone gave the announcements from the bulletin. Kat wondered what she would think about this morning to pass the time. It was the pastor's job to use his words to tug at people's hearts, and she didn't want to be manipulated. She had been a victim of that too many times. So she thought about Chloe and how she missed her. She would get to see her next weekend. What could they do to make her weekend special?

However, without realizing it, Kat found herself listening to the pastor. He was reading from Mark 1:40-42 from the Amplified Bible.

"And a leper came to Him, begging Him and falling on his knees before Him, saying, *'If you are willing, You are able to make me clean.'* Moved with compassion [for his suffering], Jesus reached out with His hand and touched him, and said to him*, "I am willing; be cleansed."* The leprosy left him immediately, and he was cleansed [completely healed and restored to health.]

"The leper had faith that Jesus could heal him, but he questioned if Jesus was willing. I think we can relate to that uncertainty. We know God can heal or deliver us from our current situation, but we don't know if He's willing. Jesus was willing, and He healed the man. He is willing to heal you and deliver you as well. The question is, are you willing to let Him? You may say yes, absolutely, I am willing. But He doesn't do things the way we do. His ways are much higher and more significant than ours because He knows the future. So, you may say yes, but are you willing to let Him do it His way?

"Another point, though, is due to this man's leprosy and having no cure, Lepers were cast out. They had to live in seclusion to prevent others from catching it. This man had been separated from his family and friends. He had felt and been alone for only God knows how long. It could have been weeks or many years since he had his last kiss, hug, or absolutely any physical touch or affection from anyone. Yet this passage says that Jesus reached out and touched him, and the leprosy left him. Jesus healed many people in various ways. Sometimes people would touch Him and be healed. Other times, Jesus would speak the words and people would be healed. However, on this particular occasion, and by no coincidence, Jesus reached out and touched this man who was most likely starving for human touch. Jesus met two needs with a single action. If you let God, He can heal and deliver you from whatever keeps you up at night and steals your peace and joy. He can heal you of every hurt and from all of your suffering. It may not be in the time and way you think it should happen, but His way is so much better than ours. He is willing. You must ask yourself, are you willing to let Him?"

Kat's heart was beating out of her chest. Tears trailed down her cheeks.

She had always wanted God to deliver her from her circumstances, but she had never been willing to let Him do it His way. She felt moved to go to the altar and yet terrified to do so. Everyone she had ever trusted had failed her. She had always kept God at arm's length for fear that He wouldn't want her and would fail her too.

Overwhelmed with emotion, she sprinted out of the church and got into her car. She drove and drove all over town, sobbing, as the pastor's words and the love she had seen in Nathan, Ms. Rose, Nathan's family, the Murrys, and even Bridgette swirled around in her mind. She was crying so hard that she was completely unaware of her surroundings until she ended up in Ms. Rose's driveway two hours after church.

Kat sat in her car, hands gripping the steering wheel hard.

She knew what she had to do. She slowly got out of the car and walked to the front door. Within seconds, Ms. Rose was there. This time, her demeanor was different.

They looked at one another, and Kat broke down.

Ms. Rose took her into her arms and held her. "Are you ready to give your life to Jesus? He loves you so much, and He always has. It's not His fault that people have hurt and abused you repeatedly in your life, but I can promise you because His word promises that He will use all of it for your good. I don't know how or when, but one day, you will look back and see."

The two women walked into the house and knelt in front of the sofa, and Kat repeated a prayer after Ms. Rose. After the words left her mouth, she cried again. The emotion felt much different this time, however. For the first time in her entire life, the dark, empty well inside her was filled with belonging and unconditional love. She felt clean and pure—and a peace she didn't know even existed.

She was truly changed.

Kat stood to her feet. "I have to see Nathan. He needs to hear it from me."

Ms. Rose nodded with a huge smile on her face.

She stood on the porch and waited. Nathan opened the door. As soon as he saw she had been crying, he took her hands into his. "What's wrong? Are you and Chloe okay?"

She smiled the most beautiful smile he had ever seen. "I just left Ms. Rose's house. I gave my life to Jesus. I wanted you to be the first person I told."

He immediately embraced her. When he pulled back, what she saw took her breath away. This tall, muscular man had tears flowing down his cheeks.

"I can't tell you how happy I am. I've been praying for you since the night we met."

Wiping tears from her eyes again, she said, "I want to thank you for everything. Not only did you save my life, but you led me to the One who has now saved my soul."

"I'm only the vessel He chose to use. He is the one who truly should get all the praise."

Nathan's gaze drew her in. There was a longing that hadn't been there before. Something had always sizzled between them, but now it was so much more. A feeling she had never felt, even with Justin.

Nervousness caused her to look away. "I should be going. I'll see you on Wednesday at Bible study."

He smiled. "I look forward to it."

Nathan stood on his porch and watched her get into her car. His feelings for her had been growing since they met, but he had never contemplated giving in to them because she wasn't a Christian. His faith was the core of him. It would never have worked out if she couldn't accept all of him, especially the most crucial part. But now that was no longer an issue.

Now the only thing keeping him from giving in to his feelings was a concern for how she still felt about Justin.

Before she drove off, he held up his hand and motioned for her to stop. She rolled down her window.

"Hey, I still owe you a Valentine's Day dinner. What are you doing tomorrow evening?"

She smiled. "I guess I'm going to dinner with you. Since we're not really dating, we can call it an outing between two friends."

"Sure, or we can call it a mock date. I'll show you how a man should treat a lady."

She giggled.

A heat wave rushed through his body. He loved her laugh. "I'll pick you up around six."

Chapter Sixteen

Kat opened the door with anticipation when she heard the knock.

Nathan stood there with a charming smile. He held out a dozen yellow roses. "These are for you."

"Thank you." She smelled them and put them on her kitchen counter. "I'll put them in a vase and water when I get back."

Nathan held out his arm. She flashed a grin, and she took hold of it. He walked her out to his car, which she noticed had been recently washed, waxed, and detailed. She tried to tame her giddy smile as he opened the car door for her but was unsuccessful.

"Where are we off to?"

"Johnathan's Grill and Bar."

"Ah, a mix between nice and casual. Good choice."

"You've been there before?"

"Only once."

He winced.

"It wasn't with Justin," she rushed to assure him. "My friend Elaina took me a couple years ago after Justin forgot my birthday."

"The more I hear about this guy, the less I like him."

She laughed. "I guess that makes two of us."

"I'm glad you have such a good friend."

"She's the best. She's always been there for me. Other than Chloe, she's the closest thing I have to family. I need to introduce you to her. She wants to meet you."

"Hopefully because she's heard such wonderful things," Nathan said with a wink.

"Maybe," she responded with a playful smile.

It was a weekday, and the restaurant wasn't crowded, so Nathan and Kat were seated quickly. Nathan pulled out Kat's chair for her before he sat down.

"You don't have to do all this. It's not like it's a real date."

"I would do all of this for you, date or not. It's how you treat a lady."

"A lady?"

"Yes, a lady."

"You are a bit old-fashioned, but that's okay. I kind of like it."

"If this were a date, I would tell you how beautiful you are and that I feel like the luckiest man in the world to be sitting here with you tonight."

"And if this were a date, I would say that you look pretty good yourself, and I feel very fortunate to be here with you."

His gaze held her captive until the server arrived.

After the server took their order and left, Nathan asked, "Is now a good time to ask why you wanted to be a nurse?"

Kat shrugged her shoulders. "I guess now is as good as ever." She hesitated for a second. Her demeanor shifted to a resemblance of a child about to take off a band-aide and expose a wound. "When I was a little bit older than Chloe, I had been left home alone for hours. I was scared and hungry. My mom, as usual, was at the bar. When she finally came home, she was with a man. She was so sloppy drunk she could barely walk. She plopped down on the couch and was hardly conscious. I was so angry with her. I screamed out, 'Where have you been? You left me alone again!' This man, who was as drunk as her, pushed me so hard against the wall that it made a big crash. Instantly I felt piercing pain throughout my left arm, and I began to scream and cry in pain. He shouted at me to shut my mouth, and then he smacked me across the face a few times, bloodying my lip. Apparently, one of the neighbors heard it and called the police because they showed up after a few minutes and took me to the hospital.

"There was the kindest nurse there. I still remember her name, Rebecca. She gave me a popsicle and told me everything would be all right. She stayed with me the entire time, even though her shift was over. She waited outside for me when they took the X-rays and was there when I came out. She held my hand while they put on my cast. She was the first one to sign it. 'You are destined for great things. Hang in there.' That was what she wrote. She even waited with me until the social worker picked me up to take me to my new placement. While I was at that placement, she sent me cards and gifts every so often. When my mom got me back several months later, we lost contact. It's because of her that I wanted to be a nurse. Since that day, I too wanted to be that person who was there for a child or adult who came in hurt, alone, and scared."

"Is being a nurse still a dream for you?"

"I don't know. I've been so focused on Justin and Chloe that I haven't thought about what I want."

"Maybe it's time you start. What you want is important too. I agree with Rebecca. You are destined for big things."

Kat wiped her mouth and placed her napkin on the table. "That was delicious. Thank you for bringing me here. If this were a date, I would let you pay."

"Oh, no, I'm paying. I invited you. This is on me. If this were a date, I wouldn't tell you that you have a speck of pepper stuck between your front teeth."

She laughed and covered her mouth, trying to remove it. "So, if we were on a date, you would let me walk around with food stuck between my teeth?"

He shrugged, "I wouldn't want to embarrass you."

She playfully threw her napkin at him.

After a delightful evening, Nathan walked Kat to her door. "Would you like to come in?"   "Thank you for the offer, but we both have to work in the morning."

His eyes searched hers, and her lips craved his.

"If this were a real date, I would kiss you. I guess this will have to do." He leaned down and kissed her cheek. Her body flushed with heat. "Goodnight, Katarina. It was fun. Perhaps I can take you on a real date sometime."

"Perhaps."

She watched him as he walked to his car. Her lips still craved his even when he was far out of sight.

Chapter Seventeen

Kat couldn't stop thinking about Nathan and their date. The more time she spent with him, the more she liked him and wanted to be around him. When she wasn't with him, a part of her felt like something was missing. She had to get him off her mind.

She got up from her desk and walked around her office. She still found it hard to believe she had such a good job. What she once thought was only coincidence or fate, she now knew was God's goodness. He had given her this job and a new apartment. She was excited that it was Friday and she would pick up Chloe in a few hours. She couldn't wait to tell her that she had given her life to Jesus.

Kat heard the door open in the lobby, and an attractive woman in her mid-thirties walked in. She had flawless brown skin. Her hair was in long braids partially up on the sides. She looked familiar, like a celebrity. Kat was sure she had seen her before on television. As she walked toward Kat, she smiled. Her teeth were exceptionally white and perfect. Perhaps she'd seen her in a toothpaste commercial.

Kat stood up and shook her hand. "Hello. What brings you in today?"

"I was wondering if you do two-month leases."

"We do. It's more cost-effective to do six months or a year, but we can do monthly leases. We also have furnished and unfurnished units available. How many bedrooms are you looking for?"

"I'm not sure. I am here for a friend. Right now, I'm going around to different places to get information. He's putting a lot of trust in me to find him a place to live for a couple months. He's coming for work."

"Well, I live here, and I can personally vouch that it's a wonderful place to live. It's well-kept, quiet, and has plenty of parking spaces. Can I show you around?"

"Yes, please."

Kat opened her desk drawer, pulled out some keys, and walked around her desk. "I'm Kat."

"I'm Yalonda Grace."

Kat's eyes lit up. "I've seen your commercials! You're a child custody attorney. I've wanted to call and set up an appointment with you so many times."

"Why haven't you?"

"I knew I wouldn't be able to afford you."

"What's your situation?"

"A few months ago, my ex-boyfriend of six years found someone else, kicked me out of our home, and now has our daughter. He only lets me have visits every other weekend."

"Why haven't you fought for her?"

"I haven't had the money. He was the breadwinner. I've only recently gotten this job. I've been saving up to get a lawyer. He tells me I should be grateful I get to see her as much as I do."

Yalonda pulled out a card from her purse. "I can easily get you full custody of your daughter. Here. Call and set up an appointment."

"But I..."

She interrupted, "I'll make sure you can afford it."

"Thank you so much," Kat said as she took the card.

For the first time since she'd moved out, she finally had a sliver of hope that she would see Chloe more often. Out of everything that had transpired over the past several months, and as hard as it had been, the thing that had been the hardest, to the point of almost unbearable, was being away from her daughter.

"Thank you, God. I know You are the one who sent her here today," Kat whispered under her breath as they walked out to look at an apartment.

As she got out of her car and walked to the door, she felt two inches taller than the last time she had been there. The door opened, but for the first time in a while, it wasn't Chloe who answered. It was Justin.

"Where's Chloe?"

"My mom's in town. She's spending the week with her. They are out shopping."

"Oh, now that I'm out of the picture, your mom wants to finally have something to do with her granddaughter?"

Justin gave her an unreadable look.

"So why didn't you call or text me and let me know instead of allowing me to waste my time and gas coming here?"

"I wanted to speak with you face to face. I told you I don't want my daughter to be around some man, a stranger that I don't know. I don't want him to have any influence on raising my daughter. I warned you, Kat, that if you kept bringing Chloe around the men you're dating, I wouldn't let you see her anymore. Now I'm keeping my word."

"Oh, so what you're saying is that you don't want me to do what you have done to me. You brought in a woman to live in my house with my daughter and influence her morning, noon, and night, with the exception of two weekends a month, but that's okay because it's you. But I'm not supposed to see anyone or move on, right? What threatens you so much, Justin? Is it that he's a man or a better man than you?"

"I think it's time for you to leave and never come back."

Kat pulled out the card from her back pocket. "I talked to Yalonda Grace today. She said she could get me full custody of Chloe. All I have to do is call her, and she will make it happen. Unlike you, I will give you a choice. We can do this civilly without lawyers, or I can get her involved with a single phone call. Come to think of it, I could probably even get some child support. It's your choice. But this is *my* weekend with Chloe. I will be back at six to get her for the weekend. Your mom has waited five years; she can wait two more days. After that, I will be back next Sunday to pick her up for the week. From now on, I get her every other week instead of every other weekend."

Kat left without waiting for his rebuttal.

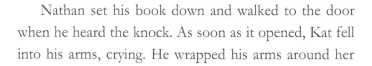

Nathan set his book down and walked to the door when he heard the knock. As soon as it opened, Kat fell into his arms, crying. He wrapped his arms around her and held her tight, breathing in her pleasant scent of clean linen and soap. It felt so natural to have her in his arms. "Are you okay, Katarina? What's wrong?"

She pulled out of his embrace. "A lawyer came into my office today, and I talked to her about Chloe. She said she could help me get custody. Today was my day to pick her up for our weekend visit. When I got there, Justin informed me that she wasn't there and that I'm not allowed to see her anymore because I didn't listen to him by allowing her to be around you, a stranger. I told him what the lawyer said and that this is my weekend to see her, and that I will be back to pick her up in an hour. I also told him I will get her every other week from now on."

"You finally stood up to him. That's fantastic. I'm proud of you. I know that wasn't easy to do. So why the tears?"

"I'm scared that he won't let me have her."

"Well, if he doesn't, you will follow through on what you said." She nodded, but with uncertainty. "Would you like me to go with you to pick her up?"

"You would do that?"

"Absolutely. It's about time I meet Justin. I don't want to be a stranger."

She giggled.

"We have half an hour to kill. Can I treat you to some ice cream?" asked Nathan.

"Well, you do owe me a real date. But I'll settle for ice cream, she said with a playful smile.

"I'll take you on a real date. I just don't want it to be rushed. I want to give you the kind of dinner you deserve." Heat rushed into her cheeks. "Speaking of dinner, would you and Chloe like to come over on Sunday after church?"

"Will you be the one preparing the meal?"

"I will be." Her mouth curved into a grin.

"Should I be worried?"

"Maybe a little."

She laughed. "Sure. We would love to."

Even though there was a cool March breeze, they decided to sit outside at the ice cream shop at one of the tables.

"I called my mom the other night and told her that you got saved last Sunday, She was thrilled. She said it was an answer to her prayers."

"Do you talk to your mom often?"

"I try to call her most Sundays."

"As a mother, I know that she appreciates it. There's just something about a mother's love. I remember the first time I held Chloe in my arms. It was the most amazing feeling. I instantly felt overwhelming love for her. It was the first time that I didn't feel alone in the world. Sometimes I wonder why my mom kept pulling me out of foster care. Was it because maybe she actually loved me or just that she didn't want to be alone?"

"I think it was both. People who have addictions are like people who are drowning. They live in this survival mode, waiting for their next fix. Just like someone drowning, they will pull their rescuer down with them unintentionally. That's why it's better to throw them a lifeline and leave it to them to hang onto it and decide if they will help themselves. They love their family and friends, but they are so focused on getting their fix that they become selfish. You are pretty remarkable, Katarina. To have walked away from the kind of life you had and be done with it. Many people fall into their parents' footsteps even though they don't want to."

"Now, looking back, I know it was a God thing. But even if I had followed in my mother's footsteps, I believe God would have made a way for me to get out."

A smile gleamed behind Nathan's eyes. "I believe that too."

Kat looked at her phone. "We should probably get going."

Nathan finished the last bite of his cone, and they were on their way.

Other than giving Nathan directions, Kat didn't say much. She was apprehensive about how Justin would respond. Nathan could see that she was nervous, but he didn't know what to say. As they pulled into the driveway and parked, Kat and Nathan swapped a glance. Kat let out a deep sigh. "I'm really glad you're here with me."

"There's nowhere else I'd rather be."

Just before Kat opened her car door, Chloe ran out with excitement. "Mommy! Nathan!"

Tears welled up in Kat's eyes. "Thank you, Lord!" said Kat as she rushed to Chloe and hugged her. "I'm so glad to see you. I've missed you so much."

"I've missed you too, Mommy." After hugging her mom, she ran to Nathan, who had just gotten out of the car. "I'm so glad you came too. I want you to meet my daddy."

Justin walked out, and Chloe took Nathan's hand and walked him over to her dad. Nathan reached out to shake Justin's hand. Justin, with a clenched jaw, looked at him without responding. "Hi, I'm Nathan. I wanted you to meet me so you wouldn't consider me a stranger."

Continuing to ignore him, Justin walked past him and over to Kat. "So, you'll keep the lawyers out of it if I agree that you get Chloe every other week?"

"If you keep your end of the deal, so will I."

Justin walked over to Chloe and kissed her on the forehead. "I love you, kiddo."

"I love you too, Daddy."

Nathan walked with Chloe to his car and helped her in while Kat and Justin finished talking. He tried not to eavesdrop, but he couldn't help but overhear some of their conversation.

"Do you love him?"

"What do you care? You stopped loving me a long time ago. The more I learn about love, the more I wonder if you ever loved me."

"That's not true. I..."

Kat cut him off, "Look, I'll have Chloe back on Sunday. I really do want her to get to know her grandmother."

Justin stood staring at her. He looked at her like he once had. A look she hadn't seen from him in a long time, probably since they had first started dating. However, this time it didn't phase her. Her gaze went to Nathan, who was interacting and laughing with Chole in his car. "We should be going. The clock is ticking. I only get so much time with her, and I consider every minute precious."

Nathan opened the door for her and waited as she got in, then sent a friendly nod to Justin, before getting back behind the wheel.

As he started the car and pulled out, Kat said, "I'm really sorry about how he treated you back there."

Nathan shrugged. "I've been treated worse. Besides, I don't blame him for hating me. I'm the one who gets to be here with you and Chloe."

They briefly locked eyes. Kat had known for some time, but now it was confirmed. Nathan was the one who now had her heart, and she was certain that he always would.

Chapter Eighteen

After the pastor said the closing prayer, Kat leaned down and picked up her purse. "Chloe is excited about going to your house for lunch today. Are you sure you don't want me to bring anything besides dessert?"

"No, I think I have it covered. We'll pick up some fast food if it doesn't turn out."

Kat laughed. "I love your confidence. Okay, well, I'll get Chloe, go home and change clothes, and pick up Krispy Kreme donuts for dessert."

"Sounds good."

As they walked to the doors leading into the foyer, Nathan's pace slowed as he glanced over at an attractive couple she had never seen before. The guy saw them and walked over with a smile, reaching out a hand. Nathan reluctantly shook it. The tension was tangible between

Nathan and this couple. No one had to tell Kat who these people were. Without hesitation, she took Nathan's arm and wrapped it around her.

As if jolted from a daze, Nathan said, "Oh, hey, this is Katarina."

"Hi, I'm Nicole," the woman said, holding out her perfectly manicured hand to shake Kat's.

"I'm Aiden," the man added.

"It's nice to meet you. I always like meeting Nathan's friends. We've been dating for a few months." Kat met his eyes. "I've never met anyone as wonderful as him. I feel like the luckiest girl in the world to have him in my life. He's truly one of a kind."

"We need to be going. It was nice seeing you both again," Nathan said. He took Kat's hand, and they walked briskly out of the church.

#

Nathan greeted Kat and Chloe at the door.

"I like your house," Chloe said. "It's nicer than I expected."

Nathan laughed. "I don't know if that's a good thing or a bit insulting."

"It's good."

"The bathroom is down the hall to the left. Go wash your hands, and then we can eat." Chloe took off, and Nathan stopped Kat from following her. "Hey, I wanted to thank you for stepping in at church. I always freeze up when I see them. Just when I think I've forgiven them, old feelings seem to resurface."

"No need to thank me. I know what it feels like to look the person in the eye who ripped your heart out and stomped on it and then have to pretend like it never happened. I had a vindictive motive when I said what I did. I wanted her to know what she missed out on, but I meant every word I said."

"Now that I've gotten over it, I'm glad things didn't work out between Nicole and me." "Why is that?"

"Because I wouldn't have met you." His gaze lingered on hers.

"Can we please eat now? I'm starving," said Chloe.

"Absolutely! Have a seat at the table."

"The food looks and smells delicious. I'm impressed," said Kat.

"Before you start throwing out compliments, you should taste it first."

"Where did you learn how to make pot roast?" asked Chloe.

"YouTube. I even seared it before I put it in the crock pot."

Kat laughed.

Nathan loved her smile. She had come such a long way since they first met, and so had his feelings for her. He wanted to take her into his arms then and there, but he wasn't sure how she felt about him or if she still wanted to get back together with Justin. "Would you like to say the prayer for the food, Chloe?" asked Nathan.

"Yes! Everyone bow your head." She looked at her mom and Nathan to see if they had listened, and then she bowed her head too. "Thank you, Lord, for this food Nathan cooked for my mommy and me. Please don't let it make us sick. Please change my daddy and keep him from getting so angry lately. Please let me live with my mommy again. Amen!"

"Amen. Thank you, Chloe, for praying," said Nathan.

"What did you mean about your daddy getting angry?" asked Kat.

"He and Mandy have been fighting a lot lately. He hit her again two nights ago."

Nathan went rigid. "What? He hit Mandy? Has he ever hit you?"

Kat had never seen Nathan like that. His jaw was tight, and his fists were clenched. Chloe shook her head no.

"He would never hit her," Kat said. "He only hits when he's been drinking."

"He's hit you before?"

"Only a few times. It was my fault. Because of everything I went through with my mom, I hate drinking. I was raging that he had too much to drink, and he hit me."

"A man should never hit a woman."

"Other than you and my foster dads, every man I've ever been around for any length of time has hit me."

Nathan tossed his napkin on the table and stood to his feet, "Please go ahead and eat. I need a minute." He walked out to his back porch.

After a few minutes, Kat told Chloe she would be right back and to keep eating. She stepped out to see what was bothering Nathan. He had his hands clenched so tightly onto the wood railing that she was concerned he would get a splinter. "Are you okay? What are you doing out here?"

He slowly turned around. He was so angry he was trembling. "Do you know what I would like to do to every man who has laid a finger on you?"

Confused by his question, she shook her head no.

"Let's just say it's not Christ-like. That's why I'm out here trying to cool off."

Kat took a step closer to him. "You're angry because of me?"

"Yes, Katarina. I... I care about you. The thought of someone hurting you bothers me."

Tears welled up in her eyes. Seeing her reaction, he stepped closer to her. "I don't know what to say. No one has ever cared about me like that."

He cupped her face. "I'm not just anyone, Katarina. You deserve to be loved and cherished."

With every word he spoke, his lips got closer to hers; but just before their lips touched, the back door opened.

"Are y'all going to come and eat or not? I don't want to eat by myself."

Nathan kissed Kat on the forehead, turned to Chloe, and smiled. "I apologize for being rude. You are my guests, and I left you at the table alone."

He and Kat went back inside and sat down with Chloe at the table while their feelings for one another continued to simmer.

Chapter Nineteen

"I've known you a long time, and I must say, Kat, you are like a different person. A better version of yourself."

"After I gave my heart to Jesus, something inside me changed. I don't know how to explain it. I feel clean and brand new, and I don't feel alone anymore. I wish you would come to church with me one Sunday."

"So the preacher did the impossible after all. He converted you."

"Nathan didn't convert me, but he has had a great influence on my life. He's an incredible man. I've never met anyone like him. He's caring, kind, and thoughtful. I could go on and on."

Elaina laughed. "You don't have to say any more. I already know. You're in love with him."

Kat wiped her mouth and put her napkin on the table. "I don't know if it's love. He makes me feel special, like he truly cares about me more than anyone else ever has. And he's so good with Chloe. She adores him."

"But how do you feel about him?"

She thought about the other day when he had almost kissed her on his back porch. "I love being with him more than anyone besides Chloe. I love his smile, his laugh, and..." She stopped herself. "I don't know... I can't bear the thought of ever being hurt again."

Elaina put her hand on Kat's. "Not all men are like Justin or the men your mother brought home. There are good ones out there. I truly think you found one."

Kat's phone rang. Her eyes darted to Elaina. "It's him. I'll be right back." She quickly stood up and walked outside to talk.

After a few minutes, she walked back into the restaurant with a massive smile and sat back down at the table. "So...?" Elaina prompted.

"He asked me to meet him tomorrow at his parents' in Johnson City. We'll spend the night there, and then Saturday morning he wants to take me to Big Creek Falls. We'll have a picnic and do a little hiking. Then I will leave to come back and pick up Chloe for the week. He will go back to his parents to preach at their church on Sunday."

But Kat's smile slowly faded.

"What's wrong?" asked Elaina.

"For the first time in a long time, I'm happy. I'm scared that at any moment, it's all going to get ripped away, and I'll be back where I was."

Elaina took both of Kat's hands. "With all you've been through, these feelings are normal. Try to enjoy the moment and not look ahead. You deserve love and happiness more than anyone I know."

"So do you, Elaina. I wish you could find someone like Nathan. You really need to come to church with me."

Elaina's phone buzzed. She took it out of her purse. "Good thing I set the alarm. I almost forgot. Unfortunately, I've got to get going. I've got to pick up Brandon from school early and take him to his dentist appointment. Thanks again for lunch. We should do it again soon. Next time, it will be my treat. Call me on Saturday when you're on your way back. I want to hear every detail about your weekend. If I can't have the fairy tale, I want to hear everything about yours."

They hugged, and Elaina left.

Kat had butterflies in her stomach the entire drive to Johnson City. She couldn't wait to see Nathan and be in his company again. On the other hand, she questioned why she was letting herself fall for him. How could a man like him, who had only dated nice girls, ever want her?

Although she was now a Christian, she still had a past. A past that could make him not want her if he knew everything. She had never met a man who truly loved her. How could she even allow herself to think that maybe he could?

As she pulled into the driveway, she realized she had talked herself out of coming and wished she hadn't. She slowly got out of the car and opened the trunk. As she was getting her small bag, Nathan walked out and took it from her hand. "What's wrong?"

She smiled halfheartedly. "Oh, nothing. I'm a little tired."

"Would you like to lie down for a little while? It's quiet. My family's at the church. After the service on Sunday, we're having a catered meal by one of the members. They are setting up the tables and getting some things ready. I wish you could be here for it, but I know you need to get back and get Chloe. Are you sure you don't want to lie down?"

"No, I'll be fine after I move around a little."

"Are you hungry? My parents are bringing back food. They shouldn't be gone much longer."

"Really, I'm fine."

Kat followed him into the house and to the room she and Chloe had stayed in the last time they were there. He set her bag on the bed.

They stood awkwardly, looking at one another. Then Nathan took a step closer to her. Kat drew in a breath, trying to control her heart rate as he brushed her hair away from her face. Her heart beat wildly due to the look of yearning in his eyes.

"Would you like to go for a walk?" he asked quietly.

"I would love to."

His hand brushed against hers. Before taking it, he asked, "May I hold your hand?"

She smiled and nodded, admiring his old-fashioned streak. She put her hand into his, and desire rushed through her body.

Nathan led her outside, and they began to walk his parents' lake property. As they walked along, he told her stories about when he was a boy and the games he used to play. She soaked in the amazing feelings she had when she was with him. The feeling of belonging, security, and comfort. It was like being with her best friend or the other part of her she hadn't known was missing.

When they arrived back at the house, Nathan's parents were there. They greeted her warmly. She loved his family. They made her feel like she was one of them.

After dinner, Kat and Nathan helped clear the table and wash the dishes. Kat rinsed them while Nathan loaded them into the dishwasher.

"Oh, this is unacceptable," said Nathan with a boyish grin, handing Kat back a plate.

"What are you talking about?"

With a teasing smile, he showed her a tiny speck of food that hadn't washed off.

She took the bottom of his shirt and wiped the plate. "I think I got it." Then, with a playful smile, she slung some soapy water onto him. "Oh, I'm sorry. Did that get on you?"

"I see how it is," said Nathan. He put his hand into the soapy water and splashed some at her.

Laughing, she pushed him back and turned to run off.

"Where do you think you're going?" he said flirtatiously as he pulled her into his arms, wrapping them around her waist. He looked into her dark brown eyes, took his index finger, and put a soap bubble on the end of her nose. All he wanted to do at that moment was to lean down and kiss her. His heart was racing uncontrollably. Uncertain of her feelings for him, he smiled, let her go, and began loading the dishes again.

Masking her disappointment, Kat scrubbed another dish and handed it to him. She knew he had almost kissed her, and she longed for it. Why hadn't he followed through? It had to be because he knew she wasn't good enough for him. After all, he was next to perfect, and she was, well, quite the opposite.

They said little as they finished the dishes. Heaviness from their uncertainty of each other's feelings hung in the air.

When they were done, Kat walked outside onto the deck and looked out over the lake. Even though it was dark, the full moon reflected off the water, causing it to look like shimmering diamonds.

Nathan came out to join her. She looked to see who it was and then turned her gaze back to the water. "What's wrong?" he asked. "It seems like something is bothering you."

She didn't want to lie, but what was she to say? *Your flirting and brief moments of affection are breaking my heart? You need to decide how you actually feel about me,* she thought. "I'm fine. I'm just tired. Perhaps I should have taken you up on that nap earlier."

He took a step closer. He couldn't control the pull she had on him. Like the same kind of pull the moon had on the ocean. His body was drawn to her, and he craved her touch. But he resisted. He didn't want to get his heart broken again. He couldn't stop wondering if she still loved Justin. After all, he had gone into this to help her get him back. Was that something she still wanted? She hadn't told him otherwise. "I'm happy you came. I'm looking forward to showing you around Big Creek Falls tomorrow."

"I am, too," she said with a half-smile.

He took another step closer, then brushed her hair out of her face and looked into her eyes.

Not wanting to play another round of 'he loves me, he loves me not,' she broke eye contact. "I know it's a little early, but I should get to bed."

He nodded and stepped back to let her walk past him and back into the house. She didn't dare look back to confirm if that was disappointment she'd glimpsed on his face. He was convinced she still had feelings for Justin by her reaction. He should give up and choose only to be her friend.

Chapter Twenty

Kat rolled over and looked at her phone. It was only five o'clock, and there was still a while before the sun or anyone else would be up. She sighed and plumped her pillow. She wanted to go back to sleep to keep her mind off Nathan. What was his deal? Sometimes he made her feel like he wanted her, and other times it seemed like they were only friends. It was maddening, especially when her feelings for him had moved far beyond friendship.

After a while, she got up and looked out the window. She watched as sunlight crept over the lake and mountains. It was a beautiful sight to behold. If only she could watch from the balcony.

Since she was by a window, she thought it only fitting to say her morning thank you's to God. "Thank You, God, for Your beautiful creation and that I got to enjoy it this morning. Thank You for Chloe, and that I'm finally going to see her more. Thank You for Nathan and for allowing me to know such a wonderful man. A kind of man I didn't know existed. But most of all, thank You for Jesus and for saving my soul."

Kat yawned. Feeling a little sleepy, she decided to lie back down. After what seemed like only a few minutes, she woke to laughter and the smell of bacon and coffee. She listened for a minute longer to the sound of Nathan's family talking, laughing, and getting along.

Growing up, she had read about healthy families and seen a few glimpses of them as a foster child, but she had never really gotten to be part of one. She pushed back the hollow ache in her chest and joined Nathan and his family for breakfast.

Nathan seemed to notice she was exceptionally quiet. After the meal, he pulled her aside. "Are you okay, Katarina? Have I done or said something to hurt you?"

"No, it's nothing. I need to leave a little earlier today. I don't think I want to go to Big Creek Falls. Perhaps we can do it another time."

Disappointment was clear in his expression. "Okay. Can I at least take you out on the boat? I've already prepared and packed our lunches."

"Sure. I'll clean up, and then we can go."

"I'll get the boat ready. Walk down to the dock whenever."

She nodded and walked back to her room.

Nathan could hardly keep his eyes on what he was doing as he saw Katarina walking toward the boat. She had her hair pulled back in a ponytail, and her gray leggings and light blue hoodie complemented her toned figure.

He took her hand and helped her climb into the boat. Then he untied the rope, pushed the boat away from the dock, and started the engine. Trying to do whatever he could to keep her there a little longer, he took her on a ride. He found it hard to steer the boat when he only wanted to look at her. If only he could take her into his arms and tell her how he felt about her.

After convincing himself that he was only setting himself up to get hurt, he took them out into the middle of the lake and then turned off the motor.

"This will be a nice spot to eat our lunch. It hasn't been that long since we ate breakfast, but I know you're in a rush to get back home, and I want you to have lunch before you go." He grabbed the cooler he had brought and pulled out two turkey sandwiches, two bags of chips, and two bottled drinks. "It's not fancy, but it's food."

"Thank you for all of this." She took a bite of the sandwich. "It's really good. Not as good as your pot roast, but definitely a close second."

"I'm glad you're easy to please."

As they ate, Nathan kept his gaze on her. When she finished, she put the sandwich bag in the pocket of her hoodie.

"Here, I can take that," he said.

Their hands touched as she handed him her trash, and she quickly pulled her hand away. He was sure by her reaction to his touch that she didn't feel the same way about him, but his feelings were so strong he had to give it one last try. He scooted closer to her on the bench. His heart began to pound so loud he thought she might hear it. She had never looked so beautiful. He took his hand and slowly turned her face toward him. Then he kissed her softly.

Eyes wide, she quickly pulled away.

"I'm so sorry, Katarina. I shouldn't have done that." Were those tears in her eyes? "I'll never do that again. I know you've made it abundantly clear that you want to be with Justin. I've tried to hold back my feelings for you, but I'm in love with you. If you give me some time, I can accept that..."

She wrapped her arms around his neck, chin lifted, and then they kissed again. Her lips tasted like a delicacy he couldn't get enough of. Her breath against his skin was intoxicating.

As they kissed, he drank her in. After a few heart-racing moments, he paused and looked at her. Then he went back for more, pressing his lips tightly against hers.

Kat grabbed the end of his shirt and started to pull it up.

Nathan pulled away from her. "I need to stop." With a breathy sigh he said, "You deserve a gentleman."

She tilted her head and gave him a sarcastic look. "I have a child. You know that I'm not..."

"You are a new creation, Katarina. You have a clean slate." She rolled her eyes, but he continued, "When I marry, no matter what happens, it will be for life. I want to give the woman I marry all of me. I've never been with a woman."

"Aren't you twenty-seven?"

"I'll be twenty-eight next month. As much as I want and desire you, I'm saving myself for the woman I marry."

Kat stared at him for a long moment, eyes wide, and filled with hurt. She quickly dropped her gaze. Regret tugged at her heart. Kat felt like she had been hit in the stomach. She knew she wasn't good enough for him, but at that moment, she realized she would never be; there could never even be a chance. Not wanting him to see the tears, she looked at her phone. "I should be getting back. I need to be on time to pick up Chloe."

Nathan nodded and started the boat. He pulled her close and put his arm around her waist as he drove back to the dock. She knew they were now a couple to him, but to her, all hope of them ever being together was gone.

He helped her out of the boat and tied it to the dock and walked her to her car. Luckily, she had already loaded her things before they went out on the water. He opened her car door and pulled her into him, running his hands down the small of her back. The feel of his skin next to hers was exhilarating.

He leaned down to kiss her again, but something was off. Kat was stiff against him, as if withdrawing behind the mental walls he thought he'd knocked down. As he leaned down, she tried to brace herself that this would be their very last kiss. The crushing feeling in her chest was overwhelming. She was in love with him, but because of her great love for him, she could never let him settle for someone like her. She smiled halfheartedly and got into her car.

He closed her door and said through the open window, "I'll come by your apartment when I get home on Sunday."

She shot him a quick smile and nodded.

Nathan watched as she pulled away.

Kat broke down crying as soon as she was out of sight. She had never loved or been loved by anyone the way she loved and was loved by Nathan. Yet because of his innocence, she knew they could never be together. She knew God had removed her sin, but her flesh was still tainted. Her purity had been stripped from her as a young girl, and if she had any left, she had given it away to Justin. Nathan deserved someone pure, like him. Someone like Bridgette.

Her vision was blurry from the constant flow of tears. She pulled off the road to calm down before getting back on the road again.

Her phone buzzed. It was a text from Justin asking if they could meet for dinner on Friday night at the same steak house they always went to celebrate. He said he had broken things off with Mandy. He wanted a new start and for them to be a family.

Kat sighed. If only this text could have come several months ago, before she ever met Nathan. Every man she met would pale in comparison. Even though she knew that she and Nathan could never be a couple, her heart would always belong to him.

She slammed the steering wheel with the palm of her hand. Why did her life always have to seem like a cruel joke?

Chapter Twenty-One

A knock sounded at the door, and Chloe yanked it open with excitement. "Nathan! I've missed you!" She jumped into his arms.

"Hey, Chloe girl. You've grown since the last time I saw you. Where's your mom?"

When Kat heard his voice, warmth rushed through her body. More than anything, she wanted to run into his arms and feel his lips against hers again. But that wasn't an option. She hated what she was about to do.

When her composure was in place, she walked out into the living room. Nathan's face lit up when he saw her, but she gave him a serious look. "Can we go outside to talk?" She looked at Chloe. "I need you to straighten your room while I talk to Nathan."

Chloe gave her a frustrated look.

"Listen to your mother," said Nathan kindly.

As soon as they walked outside, Nathan pulled her into his arms. He sighed deeply. "I've missed you so much. I haven't stopped thinking about you. I couldn't wait to see you and hold you again."

Kat pulled away with tears in her eyes.

"What's wrong, Katarina?"

She couldn't look into his eyes. She knew what she had to say would hurt him, but she would rather hurt him now than later, when he regretted everything.

"Please tell me."

"I... I heard from Justin on my way home from your parents' house Saturday. We are meeting for dinner on Friday. He wants to get back together."

His jaw tightened. "After all he's done to you, you're actually considering it? What about us? Can you honestly say that you don't have feelings for me?"

She knew if she told him the real reason—that she wasn't, nor would she ever be, good enough for him—he would talk her out of it. He would say it was in her past and to leave it there. But he deserved purity. He deserved someone like him, innocent and able to give the woman he married all of him without baggage. She could never have those qualities. She could never give him what he deserved. She was tainted, broken, and scarred.

"I have to think about Chloe. I have to give her what I never had... a family."

The look on his face made her heart feel like it was breaking into pieces. But she was doing the right thing. Even though it hurt now, it would save them both from even greater heartache later.

She reached into her back pocket and pulled out an envelope. "I don't think we should see each other anymore. I've tried to keep track of the money you've given me over the past several months. I may be slightly off, but I think it's close."

Tears fell down Nathan's cheeks. "I never wanted you to repay me."

"I always intended to."

"I don't want your money. Please, Katarina, don't do this. I love—"

She cut him off before he could finish. "I will never be able to thank you for all you've done for Chloe and me. You've been there for me like no one else. You literally saved my life, and because of your influence, my soul too."

Seeing the tears she had caused and his expression made her want to cave in and take back everything she had said. But she kept remembering a sermon she had recently heard about love and how genuine love required sacrifice. She truly loved Nathan, and because of that love, she would sacrifice what she wanted for what was ultimately best for him, even if that meant them not being together and him being with someone else.

"Can I say goodbye to Chloe?"

Kat opened the door and called for her.

Chloe walked out. "What's wrong, Nathan?"

He knelt to be at eye level with her. "Your mom and I won't be seeing each other anymore. I didn't want to leave without saying goodbye."

Chloe darted a look of anger at her mother. "Mommy!"

As he watched Chole's lip quiver, tears began to fill Nathan's eyes again. "You are such a special little girl," Nathan told her. "Getting to know you over the past several months has been such a blessing. I know God has big plans for you. I will never forget you. You will always be in my prayers."

Chloe wrapped her arms around his neck and held him tightly. They both cried as he held her.

After a long moment, Kat told Chloe it was time to let go.

Chloe glared at her mother, a look Kat had never seen from her. "I will never forgive you for this."

"Chloe, please don't be angry with your mother. She loves you and has your best interest at heart."

"No she doesn't," she shouted. "If she did, she would never make me say goodbye to you!"

"Go inside, Chloe," Kat said quietly. "We'll discuss this later."

Crying, Chloe stomped inside and to her room.

Nathan handed Kat the envelope of money. She held up her hand and shook her head no, but he pressed it into her palm. "Use this to help someone else."

She took it from his hand. "I'm so sorry, Nathan. You will see one day that this is best for everyone."

"I'm not so sure about that." Nathan turned to walk away, but with grief in his eyes, he stopped and looked back at her. "If Justin hurts you again, which I suspect he will, I will still be here for you, Katarina. My feelings won't change. Even if you don't love or feel the way I do about you, I will always be here for you."

She nodded as tears filled her eyes. "Thank you."

His pining gaze lingered on hers for another second, as if trying to take in every detail of her. Then he turned and walked away.

Every step he took that put distance between them, made her feel like she couldn't breathe. She went straight to her bedroom, fell onto her bed, and cried like she had when she was a little girl and felt like all hope was gone.

Chapter Twenty-Two

Kat walked into Remington's Prime Steakhouse in downtown Nashville. It was the place Justin had taken her to when they were dating and for special occasions. Kat scanned the room, looking for him in the crowd. They had driven separately at her request. Memories flooded her as she took in the familiar scenery. This was where Justin had told her that he loved her for the first time. It was also where he told her he had bought them a house and that he wanted them to be a family.

She spotted him sitting at a table near the entrance. When he saw her, he stood and waved for her to join him. He kissed her cheek and helped her get seated.

"You look gorgeous. Thank you for coming." His pupils widened with a look of desire for her. That look had once made her knees weak. For so long, she had longed for him to look at her like that again, even before he kicked her out. But now, this look meant nothing to her. All she could think about was Nathan. Justin wasn't half the man he was. After feeling what true love felt like, she would never have feelings for Justin or anyone else.

Kat was relieved when the server came. After telling him what they wanted, Kat's phone buzzed. It was Ms. Rose. She probably wanted to know what had happened between her and Nathan. Now wasn't the time to tell her. Kat slipped her phone back into her purse. "So, what did you want to talk to me about?"

Justin took Kat's hands. "You know my job had me move here several years ago from California. All of my family still live there. Well, now they are moving me back. I'm leaving next week. I'm selling the house, and I want you and Chloe to come with me. As I said in my text, I want us to be a family. I was a fool to let you go, and I want to make things right. What do you say?"

Kat blinked hard. "First of all, I'm a Christian now, Justin. I will never play house again. If I live with a man, we will be married. Second, you expect me and Chloe to drop everything—her school, my job—and leave with you next week?"

"I promise we will marry after we get settled in. Look at it as a new start."

"What about Mandy?"

"What about Mandy? Things are over between us. I've given her a couple of weeks to collect her things from the house and to move out."

"You must be getting more generous. You only gave me a week. Of course, you also proposed to her and never did to me."

"You are the woman I want. I have always wanted to marry you. I gave her more time because of the baby."

"Baby! Is it yours?"

"She says it is, but with a woman like her, who really knows?"

Kat removed her hands from his. "How can you look into your daughter's eyes when you treat women so horribly?" She stood. "Neither Chloe nor I will be joining you. I want nothing to do with you now or ever."

"You've changed a lot, Kat. At one time, you would have followed me anywhere."

"Well, unfortunately, Justin, you haven't changed at all." She marched out of the restaurant, hoping never to see him again.

The following day, Kat took the day off. She dropped Chloe off at school and went to Justin's to pack up Chloe's things. When she pulled into the driveway, she saw Mandy's car. She knocked on the door and turned the knob. It was open, so she walked in. There were boxes everywhere. It reminded her of when she and Justin had first moved in. They were so excited about the baby growing inside her and their new life together. She never dreamed it would turn out like this.

Kat heard crying coming from the master bedroom—the bedroom she had shared with Justin and he had shared with Mandy. She stood at the door and found Mandy on her knees, sobbing, surrounded by photos.

Kat's heart was filled with compassion. She knew exactly how she felt. She felt rejected, unloved, scared, and full of uncertainty.

Mandy looked at her over one shoulder, clearly embarrassed. She wiped her face with the back of her hand and quickly started sorting. "I'm sure you're thrilled to see me like this."

"Not in the least. I wouldn't wish what you're feeling on anyone." Kat kneeled beside her and put her arm around her shoulders. "I know it doesn't seem like it now, but you will be okay."

Mandy turned and threw her arms around Kat, crying even harder. Kat couldn't help but cry with her.

After a while, Mandy let go and wiped her face with her hands. "I'm so sorry, Kat, for all the pain I caused you and all that Justin and I put you through. I was so clueless."

"I have already forgiven you and Justin."

"I don't know what I'm going to do or where I'll go."

"Do you have a family?"

She shook her head. "I am an only child. I never knew my father, and my mother said she wouldn't help raise a child made out of wedlock."

Kat remembered the envelope of money Nathan wouldn't take. He had told her to use it to help someone else. She could use it to help Mandy. "With a few conditions, you can live with Chloe and me until you can get on your feet and get your own place. I have a three-bedroom apartment. You can have your own room."

"You would do that for me?"

Kat nodded.

"Why?"

"A few months ago, I never would have made this offer or had the least bit of compassion for you, but I became a Christian. I'm a new person. It all came about because someone showed me compassion and helped me when I was at my lowest. Now I get to do the same for you."

"What are your conditions?"

"Every day while you're living with us, I want you to get up every morning and thank God for at least five things."

Mandy gave her a questioning look.

"I know it sounds ridiculous, but someone told me to do this, and it helped me when I was where you are. The next thing is to read a chapter or a section from the Bible every day. Do you have a Bible?"

"I have my grandmother's old Bible."

"And the last thing is, you must go to church with Chloe and me every Sunday. Trust me, I know all of this sounds crazy, but it actually helps."

Mandy thought about it for a second. She didn't seem keen on the idea, but she didn't have much of a choice. "Okay, I'll do it, and I promise not to wear out my welcome. I'll try to be out before the baby is born."

"How far along are you?"

"Four months."

"Is that why Justin proposed to you?"

She nodded and then began to cry again.

"It will be okay. You'll get through this, and I will help you every step of the way."

With tears streaming down her face, Mandy smiled. "Thank you."

Kat grabbed a few empty boxes. She went into Chloe's room and packed up all her things, denying the memories that tried to creep in and cause tears. Now wasn't the time for nostalgia. She needed to get the job done and be on her way.

Before she left, she handed Mandy a piece of paper with her address. "We have dinner at five. You're welcome to come whenever."

"Are you sure about this?" asked Mandy.

"I am. I want to help you. Besides, the baby you're carrying is Chloe's baby brother or sister."

"Brother," Mandy said sadly. "Chloe doesn't know about him yet. We never told her. We didn't know how she would take it."

"Well, you can do that tonight. I think she'll be very excited."

"Thank you, Kat. I don't know what to say. This means so much to me."

Kat smiled. "I know because I've been there."

A little while later, Kat left to pick up Chloe from school. When Chloe got in the car, she didn't say anything. She had barely spoken to her since she had broken things off with Nathan.

"How was your day?"

"Fine."

"Are you hungry?"

"No."

"Do you have homework?"

"Yes."

"I'll help you with it when we get home. After that, we can go to the park if you'd like. We haven't been in a while."

Chloe didn't respond.

"I saw Mandy today when I went to collect your things from your dad's house. Your father has done the same thing to her that he did to me. He kicked her out. She has no place to go, so she'll stay with us for a while until she can find a place to live."

"What! Where is she going to stay?"

"In the guest room. She needs help, just like I once did. I intend to be there for her the same way..." She trailed off.

"The same way Nathan was for you," Chloe finished.

"I have forgiven her. So can you."

Chloe folded her arms over her chest and stubbornly stared out the window.

As soon as they arrived at the apartment, Chloe got out, slammed her door, and went straight to her room.

Kat knocked on her door and waited, but she didn't respond, so she let herself in. Chloe was lying on her bed with her face buried in her pillow. "Why are you acting like this? Does it have to do with your father moving away or Mandy moving in with us?"

Chloe lifted her head. "Nathan! You said we would discuss it, and we never have. Why did you stop dating him? He was so nice and good to us. Why don't you love him?"

"It's complicated. I'm not sure how to explain it."

"Well, try."

Kat sighed and sat down beside Chloe. "Okay, here goes. Do you know what a gem is?"

"Yeah, we learned about them in school. It's a very special stone."

"In a way, everyone is born with a priceless gem. You're supposed to give it to the one you marry. Once you give it away, you can never get it back. Well, my gem was stolen from me when I was a young girl, not much older than you, by one of the men my mother brought home when she was drunk. Even if I still had it, I would have given it to your father. So, my gem is far gone. You see, Nathan still has his gem. If we stayed together and one day married, it would be natural for him to give me his gem, but I don't have mine to give to him. It's not fair to him. He deserves someone who can give one back to him. To answer your question, I do love him more than I have loved anyone other than you. But it's because I love him that I can't be with him. If I could go back in time and change all of it, I would. I would have saved my special gem for only him. But I can't. What I can do is stay out of his life so that he can find someone else. I want him to find someone who can give him what he deserves. Does that make sense?"

Chole shrugged, "kind of." Chloe scooted closer to her mother and hugged her. "I'm sorry your special gem was stolen from you, Mommy."

Kat's eyes filled with tears. "So am I. I will do everything in my power to make sure that yours never is. I hope and pray that you learn from me and wait to give your special gem away to the person you marry. A person who truly loves and cares about you like Nathan did about me."

Chapter Twenty-Three

Kat held back tears as she drove Mandy and Chloe to their new church. All she wanted to do was keep driving to New Life Hope, their haven over the past several months. It was mainly because Nathan and Ms. Rose were there, but she knew finding another church would be better for everyone. She longed to see Nathan standing in the foyer waiting on her before they entered the sanctuary, or Ms. Rose greeting her with a warm smile and tight hug.

Although it was difficult, she was doing the right thing. Her heart couldn't take seeing Nathan and not being able to be with him and, even worse, watching him move on with Bridgette or someone else.

She tried to keep her thoughts positive. Today was about new beginnings. This would be a chance for her,

Chloe, and Mandy to find a new refuge and church family.

But no matter how hard she tried, the ache of missing Nathan always seemed to creep in.

Kat looked over at Mandy. She was ghost white and was wringing her hands. "Are you okay?"

"I'm trying to prepare myself for the stares, smirks, and whispers as I walk in, pregnant and unmarried."

Kat smiled at her. "Once again, I know exactly what you are feeling. It will be okay. If I've learned anything over the past several months, it's that Jesus came for the broken, like you and me. If these people are true Christians, they will welcome us with open arms. But regardless of what happens, you're not alone. We are in this together. We can look for another church if we need to."

As she pulled into the much smaller parking lot next to the much smaller church than they were used to, Chloe sighed with disappointment. "I miss Nathan and our old church. Why can't we go there?"

"I've already explained it to you, Chloe. For now, we're giving this church a try. It being smaller might make it easier to make more friends."

"There won't be as many kids to make friends with."

Mandy looked over at Kat. "She's no dummy. She definitely takes after you."

Kat laughed. "I probably shouldn't, but I agree with you."

They all got out of the car, each apprehensive in their own way. As they walked in, Mandy followed Kat closely as if she were her second child. They were instantly greeted by an older gentleman who stood at the door with a huge smile. He shook all three of their hands and handed them a program. They walked through double doors into a small sanctuary with a single center aisle.

This would be the perfect church to be married in.

Kat quickly dismissed the thought. She sat on a pew in the back, and Chloe and Mandy sat beside her. This church smelled and looked newly renovated. Most of the people were older, but there were a few people around her and Mandy's age, most of them married with families. They stood out. But standing out wasn't always bad, and she refused to make it out to be.

A nice older woman with gray curly hair approached them. "We are so glad you're here with us today. My name is Mary."

Kat shook her hand. "I'm Kat, this is my daughter Chloe, and this is our friend Mandy."

"It is very nice to meet all of you. After the music, I take the children to the back and teach a lesson; we do a craft and have a snack." She looked at Chloe. "Would you like to join us today?"

Chloe nodded enthusiastically.

"Okay. After the music, listen for the pastor to release the children and follow the others back."

The music began, and Mary quickly returned to her seat. The worship leader asked everyone to stand and take out a hymnal from the back of the pew. This seemed vaguely familiar to Kat. At one of the foster homes she lived in, they had gone to a church that used them.

"Please turn to page one hundred seventy-nine, 'Amazing Grace.'"

As the congregation sang, Kat remembered hearing this song at a couple funerals she had attended, one being her mother's. She began to tear up. It wasn't because she missed her mom. It was because of the words. She had never really listened to or understood them. That was different now.

As the words, "I once was lost but now am found, was blind but now I see" left her lips, tears flowed down her cheeks. She was not on the same faith maturity level as Nathan and Ms. Rose, but she was changed forever and never wanted to be the person she'd been. Gratitude swelled in her heart as she soaked in the fact that she now was found by the One who had pursued her for her entire life. The One she had pushed aside and blamed for all the bad things that happened to her. How different would her life have been if she had surrendered to Him years ago? Regardless, she was His now, and no matter what darkness lurked around the next corner, her future would be better because He was in it.

Kat looked over at Mandy. She, too, had tears in her eyes. She would have never imagined a month ago that she would actually consider Mandy a friend and that they would sit next to each other in church. But here they were. Kat remembered what Ms. Rose had said the day she gave her heart to Jesus—that God would use all the bad things in her life for good. If God could use all the abuse, rejection, hopelessness, and brokenness to bring someone else to Jesus, then it would all be worth it. He had been so good to her, even before she gave Him the credit.

After the music, the pastor released the children. Chloe anxiously followed the other children, and Kat and Mandy sat down. Hurt spread in her chest as she remembered what it felt like to sit beside Nathan, how her stomach would get butterflies when she would brush up against him. The last Sunday they were at church together, he put his arm around her. She loved the feeling of his touch.

Part of her hoped he would move on and soon pursue Brigette. They would be so perfect together. But the other part of her felt sick at the very thought. She took a deep breath, trying to put it out of her mind. He was off the table for her; them being together would never be an option.

She glanced over at Mandy. She had a sheepish look on her face, yet she was listening intensely to the sermon. Kat assumed she was feeling the same feeling she had experienced her first few times at church. Like every word was being preached directly at her. Mandy probably felt it even stronger because it was a much smaller church, and they were the new people.

After the service, they were greeted by many of the churchgoers. All of them were nice and welcoming.

Kat smiled as they walked back to the car. She was confident that they had found their new church.

Chloe took her mother's hand. "I miss the other church, and I sure miss Nathan. But I think I'm going to like it here. Ms. Mary is really nice, and I met a new friend today. Her name is Bella. She's the pastor's granddaughter. She says she comes every week."

"That's wonderful, sweetheart. What about you, Mandy? How did you like it?"

"It was church."

Kat smiled. "Okay. We'll give it another try next week."

As they were driving home, Kat remembered she hadn't returned Ms. Rose's call from the other night when she met with Justin. She was probably wondering what had happened between her and Nathan. So much had changed since the last time they had talked, and she had much to tell her.

"Mandy, do you mind watching Chloe for a little while after lunch? I need to go and see someone."

"Not at all."

Chapter Twenty-Four

Kat finished the dishes, she let Mandy know she was leaving to go see Ms. Rose and to call if she needed her.

"I want to go, Mommy."

Kat grabbed her purse and keys and kissed Chloe on the forehead. "Not this time, sweetheart."

Chloe's shoulders went limp, and she went to her room.

As Kat drove to Ms. Rose's house, nervousness settled in her stomach. Nathan was like a grandson to her, and Kat had broken his heart. She may want nothing to do with her anymore. Although the thought saddened her, it bothered her even more for Chloe. She had lost her father, Nathan, and church only in a few days. What if she lost Ms. Rose, the only grandmother figure she had ever known?

There was a great heaviness in her chest as she knocked on the door. She waited a few minutes, but Ms. Rose didn't come. She knocked again. Tears filled her eyes as she turned to walk back to her car.

Then suddenly, she heard the door open. "Katarina! I'm so glad you've come." Ms. Rose reached out and hugged her. "I'm sorry it took so long to come to the door. I was pulling an apple pie out of the oven. Would you like some? It's nice and warm. I can pull out some vanilla ice cream to go with it."

"It's a good thing I don't visit more often, or I would weigh five hundred pounds." Kat followed her into the kitchen and sat at her small kitchen table. Ms. Rose put a warm piece of apple pie and a scoop of ice cream in front of her. The pleasant aroma made her mouth water. "Thank you. You don't always have to feed me. I come here to see you, not eat your food."

"Nonsense. So tell me, what happened between you and Nathan? He seemed upset this morning. He sat in his usual spot and he kept looking over to where you usually sit. After a few minutes, he got up and walked to the back of the church. Noticing something was wrong, I joined him and asked him if he was okay, but he said he wasn't ready to talk about it and left. I believe he spent the remainder of the service in his office. Only matters of the heart can cause that type of reaction, so I knew it had something to do with you."

Kat let out a deep sigh. Tears welled in her eyes. "It's my fault. I've hurt him. It would have been better for him if he had never met me."

Ms. Rose gave her a solemn look. "What did you do to hurt him?"

"Things changed between us after my visit to his parents' last weekend. Feelings have been brewing between us for some time, but we officially crossed the line from friends to a couple. Then he told me he.... that he has never been with a woman. So I ended things. He thinks the reason is that I was getting back with Justin. But I turned Justin down, and he's moved back to California. The truth is, I have a child. I lived romantically with a guy for years. I'm far from innocent. He deserves someone like him. Someone who can offer him what I can't."

Ms. Rose put her hand on Kat's. "I see. He's in love with you, Katarina, and you with him. He knows you aren't innocent and yet took part in moving your relationship further along. Don't you think the decision should be his? He's made it. If he's okay with it, why shouldn't you be?"

"He's blinded by love. It may not be an issue now, but I know it would be one day. Most certainly on our wedding night, if things ever got that far. I can't let him settle for someone like me. He deserves so much better.

He deserves someone like Bridgette or another nice girl from the church."

"Sweetheart, I think you are making a mistake. You're protecting yourself. I think a part of it is your fear that he will eventually reject you like your dad, mom, and Justin."

Kat shrugged. Even if Ms. Rose was right, she couldn't deny that Nathan deserved someone much better than her. She loved him too much to let him settle, no matter how much pain it caused both of them. "Please don't talk to him about me. Please encourage him to move on and find a nice girl."

"Is that what you truly want?"

Kat paused for a second. "Yes."

"Okay, but I will also pray that he ultimately ends up with whom God wants him to."

Kat nodded, knowing full well it wasn't her.

"So, what's this about Justin moving to California?"

"He sold his house and left this week. Chloe will be living with me now. He kicked Mandy out and she's four months pregnant. She has nowhere to go, so she's living with us until she can find her own place. If someone had told me a year ago that I would have voluntarily invited her to live with me, I would have told them they were delusional. What can I say? Only God can do things like that."

Ms. Rose smiled. "Isn't that the truth."

Chapter Twenty-Five

Nathan grimaced as he looked at the empty seat beside him. Another Sunday morning service without Katarina. Another day with the ache of missing her in his heart. It had been a month since the last time he heard her voice, looked into her dark brown eyes, or touched her soft, tan skin. A month that had felt more like an eternity. So many times during her counseling sessions, he had driven by the church, hoping to catch a glimpse of her. A few times, he came close to being there when she came out. But what could he say to make her want him over Justin when she had already made her choice?

After church, he went to Ms. Rose's house for lunch. He parked his car in her driveway, but waited a few minutes before going in. He found it hard to do anything lately, even the things he once enjoyed.

Ms. Rose stood at her door with a warm smile. She gave him a hug and invited him inside.

"It smells delicious. Thank you for inviting me over. Will anyone else be joining us?" he asked as he sat in his usual chair at her small kitchen table.

Ms. Rose's grin curved into a frown. She knew what he was hoping for. "It will only be the two of us today."

"Have you heard from Katarina lately?"

"She and Chloe came by a few days ago."

"How are they?"

"They are doing well. It's not been easy adjusting to all the changes, and now the baby adds another level of complexity to everything. But overall, they are doing good. I'm very proud of Katarina. She's come a long way. You are a big reason for that."

"Baby!"

"Oh, I've said too much."

Nathan felt instantly queasy. The smell that had made his stomach growl now threatened to make it empty its contents. Justin had gotten her pregnant again? What would stop him from discarding her when he found someone else? Nathan burned with anger and envy, neither an emotion he was proud of.

"She did mention you."

His head jerked up. "What did she say?"

"That she hoped you would give Bridgette a chance. She feels that she genuinely cares about you."

His head drooped again. "What do you think?"

Ms. Rose sighed. "I don't know. Love is so complicated—especially these days. I don't envy any young person trying to find love. However, God is still the same, faithful and unchanging. My only advice is to seek Him. For the record, I know that she still cares deeply for you. But she's made up her mind, and I don't know if she'll ever be available again."

Nathan didn't say much for the remainder of the meal. He tuned out Ms. Rose's voice as he thought about everything she had told him. Maybe Katarina was right about Bridgette. She had been there for him after Nicole cheated on him. She had always been considerate, encouraging, and caring. He had only ever seen her as a friend. But why? She was pretty, sweet, and like-minded as him in the things that mattered.

Soon after getting into his car to go home, Nathan took out his phone. He thumbed through pictures he had taken with Katarina and Chloe. His heart felt overwhelmed with misery. He had to move on. She had, and so must he.

His thumb hovered over Bridgette's number. Then he took a deep breath and forced himself to tap it.

"Hello."

"Hey, Bridgette. It's Nathan."

"Well, what a nice surprise to hear your voice. Is everything okay?"

"Yeah. I was wondering if you have dinner plans tomorrow."

"No," she said, surprise and excitement clear in her voice.

"Would you like to have dinner with me?"

"I would love to. What time were you thinking?"

"Would six be a good time for you?"

"I get home from work around four-thirty. That would give me a few minutes to grade some papers. That would be perfect!"

"Okay, I'll pick you up around six."

"I look forward to it."

Nathan put his phone down on the passenger seat and sighed. His heart still pined for Katarina, but at least he was taking steps to move on.

Chapter Twenty-Six

Just before Kat got out of her car to go into the church for counseling, her phone buzzed. It was a text message from Mandy, with a small list of groceries she wanted Kat to pick up from the store on her way home. It was her night to make them all dinner.

Kat sighed. She didn't mind doing it, but it wasn't uncommon for her to have mascara running down her face after her sessions. She would try her best not to cry today.

Kat sat down and tried to prepare herself. Even after several months of coming, it hadn't gotten any easier.

Linda closed the office door and sat in the chair next to her. "So, how have things been going since our last visit?"

"I can't complain."

"I've noticed in our previous sessions that you have avoided mentioning Nathan. You still must have feelings for him. I think it's something we need to discuss."

"I don't see why it's necessary. It's over. I don't, nor will I ever, have what he deserves, and that's that. It's been a couple months, so hopefully he's moved on by now."

"Do you really hope that?"

"I don't relish the thought of him being with someone else, but I genuinely want him to be happy. So yes. I hope he has."

"Do you ever think about how small your inner circle is? It's Chloe and Elaina. You've recently added Ms. Rose and Nathan. However, as soon as your feelings for Nathan became stronger and he gave you a reason that alarmed you, you pushed him out of your circle. You keep saying that you ended things because of his innocence, and I do think that is some of it. But you not feeling like you deserve him... I think it goes much deeper than that. I think you keep people at arm's length for fear they will reject and abandon you. Maybe you ended things with Nathan because you are afraid that one day, he would reject you as other people have in your life."

Kat allowed those words to sink in, and then the unwanted tears came. "You're the second person who has told me that. I think you are both right. Other than Chloe, I've never loved anyone as much as I loved

Nathan. I'm terrified by it. I couldn't bear it if our relationship grew into something more, and he didn't want me anymore. His innocence is a big issue. Why would he want someone like me when he could have someone pure and without emotional scars? I'm certain he would only regret being with me once he came to his senses."

"You must purge this way of thinking. Unfortunately, rejection is a part of life. It's not always as severe as what you've experienced, but sometimes people will hurt you, intentionally or not, simply because they are human. Look at how much you love Chloe, yet you've disappointed and hurt her before. Once again, it's because you are a human. The love of people will never be enough. People can't be where you get your worth and value. You must find that in God. His love for you is truly all you will ever need. The love of others is just a bonus. You may not like God's time frame or methods, but He will always come through, and He promised never to leave or forsake you, no matter what you do or how badly you blow it. The love of your family and friends should be only secondary to His. You must have the proper perspective, that no matter what happens or how people hurt you, your world will never be destroyed. If you don't do this, you will only weigh those you love down with a heavy weight that they can't carry. Because no matter how much they love you, it can never be enough. Only God's love can be."

Kat left the church knowing that everything Linda had said was true. Yet she didn't know how to relinquish her sole love to Jesus. Even though God had changed her and had been so good to her, a part of her worried that He, too, would one day reject her. Regardless, she knew she had to change. She never wanted to be a weight to anyone. She was very familiar with what that felt like and never wanted to be that way.

As Kat drove home, she remembered she needed to get the stuff for Mandy at the store. She made a quick turn into the Kroger parking lot, touched up her makeup, and went shopping.

In the spice aisle, she bent down to grab the dried parsley and bumped into someone. Without looking, she said, "Oh, I'm sorry."

"Kat?"

Recognizing the voice, she turned around. "Bridgette, how have you been?"

"Doing very well. We've missed you at church."

"We are going to the City of Refuge Church just down the street. After what happened between Nathan and me, I thought it would be better for everyone. I've been meaning to apologize to you but haven't found a good time to do it. I didn't mean to lie when I told you I would never hurt Nathan. Regrettably, I'm afraid I did."

"There's no need to apologize. I want to thank you for encouraging Nathan to call me. We've been seeing each other for around a month now. In fact, he's coming over tonight for dinner. That's why I'm here. I'm making homemade lasagna. His favorite."

Kat felt a pang of disappointment. Bridgette's words pierced her to her core. But she forced herself to say, "That's wonderful! I've been praying that he'd find a nice girl. I think you are a perfect match for him."

"Thank you, Kat. I'm sorry things didn't work out for the two of you. I will make the same promise I asked you to make. I will never hurt him. He means a lot to me. He's an amazing man."

Kat fought tears. Trying to find her voice, she responded, "He truly is. I've never met anyone like him. Well, I should be going. I wish you both the best."

Kat darted to the restroom and the nearest stall. Overtaken by heartache, she sobbed like the wound was fresh and new. Why was she so upset? She had prayed that he would move on and find a virtuous woman. Now he had. Her prayers had been answered. Besides, she hadn't even known lasagna was his favorite meal because when they were together, she'd been so absorbed in her own problems.

No matter how hard she tried, she couldn't stop crying.

After several minutes, she pulled herself together and wiped her face with some toilet paper. So much for avoiding mascara streaks.

Linda's words haunted her. She was right. Kat didn't end things with Nathan only because of his innocence. There was more to it. Her feelings ultimately came from the fear that he would reject her one day, and at that moment, she'd felt like he had. So instead of being rejected, she had rejected him.

Now he had moved on. It was time for her to take action to get better and do what Linda had suggested. She was so tired of being a hostage to her past. To be genuinely happy, her first love had to be Jesus.

Chapter Twenty-Seven

Nathan couldn't deny that she was beautiful. Her blonde hair was pulled back in a messy bun and her blue eyes looked soulfully into his. She had grown up in a Christian home and had an unblemished past. Besides having a nice figure, being caring and smart, Bridgette was the opposite of Katarina. She seemed like the perfect match for him in every way. They had been on four dates, and all of them had been enjoyable.

But Bridgette had one major flaw—one that he would never be able to get over.

She wasn't Katarina.

No matter how hard he tried, he couldn't get over her. He still longed for her company and touch.

"Thank you for having me over tonight," he said to Bridgette. "The lasagna was delicious. I can't believe you remembered it was my favorite. I only told you once, and that was ages ago."

She smiled. "You are important to me. If you like something, it's worth remembering." "I'm sure it's been a long week for you, wrangling all those first graders. How about you sit on the couch, prop your feet up, and rest? I'll take care of the dishes."

"Let's not worry about them now. I can do them tomorrow."

"Please, I insist. You worked all day and then cooked a nice meal for me. It's the least I can do."

"Okay... I'll pick a movie."

He took their plates, walked to the sink, and opened the dishwasher. As he was rinsing them, a smile spread across his face as he remembered doing the dishes with Katarina when they were at his parents' house and their playful interaction. The longing in her eyes that he hadn't seen before. If only he had kissed her.

That heavy, crushing weight returned to his chest. What was she doing now? Was she happy? Had Justin broken her heart once again? He swallowed hard, trying to rid himself of the fear of never seeing her again and knowing she would never be his.

Nathan dried his hands on a towel and shook the thought of Katarina from his mind. How could he be thinking of her when he was on a date with someone else?

THE SAME LAST NAME

After finishing the dishes, he sat beside Bridgette on her couch. "I don't bite," she said with a schoolgirl smile. He smiled back and scooted closer to her. She started the movie.

After a few minutes, she took his arm and wrapped it around her. "There, that's much better," she said as she nestled into him.

Guilt rushed through him and landed in the pit of his stomach. It felt like lead. He knew she was falling for him, and his feelings toward her hadn't changed. He didn't want to hurt her, especially when he had a fresh wound and knew the pain of rejection. But how could he avoid it? He couldn't continue dating her, just waiting to see if his feelings would change or by forcing himself to fall in love with her. It wasn't fair to her. She deserved better.

He went back and forth on whether he should tell her how he felt and end things between them or keep things going to see if they would change.

She looked at him and smiled flirtatiously. Then she took his hand that was resting in his lap into hers. What if her next move was a kiss? Just as he had the thought, she was tilting her chin up and leaning toward his lips.

Nathan let go of her hand and slowly stood, rubbing the back of his head.

"I'm sorry if I scared you. I suppose I was rushing things a bit," she said as she stood too.

"I'm the one who should be apologizing. I think you are an amazing woman. You are beautiful, smart, and caring. It's just that I..."

"You're in love with someone else."

He nodded. "We will probably never be together again, but I can't help how I feel about her, and that isn't fair to you."

"She's a fortunate woman to have your heart."

"I'm sorry, Bridgette. You deserve someone who feels for you the way I do about Katarina." He walked to the door and opened it.

He looked back at her, and she smiled warmly. "Maybe we will both get our happy endings one day, Nathan."

"I'm not too sure about me. But I truly hope that you do."

Chapter Twenty-Eight

Kat and Chloe passed New Life Hope church on their way to the store. Nathan was most likely there, and every part of Kat wanted to pull into the parking lot, find him, and run into his arms. But what would that accomplish? She was the same tainted woman, and he was still the same perfect man. Besides, he had moved on with someone far more suitable for him than she. Kat genuinely hoped he was happy.

Kat's mouth tightened when she saw the sign. She hoped Chloe wouldn't notice, but then she yelled from the back seat, "Mommy! Mommy! Next week is New Life's VBS. VBS stands for vacation Bible school. I want to go! Please, Mommy, can I go?"

"You know I can't take you. I can't go back there."

"Why not?"

"The church is Nathan's job. It would be awkward if I saw him. Besides, people would ask why we stopped going there. I don't think it would be right to talk about it."

"Just because you don't want to go doesn't mean I can't. You can't keep someone from going to church. Can Mandy take me?"

"She's finished her training and now has her real estate license. She starts showing houses this week, so she'll probably be too busy."

"I can at least ask. If she can, can I go? Please, Mommy? Please?"

Kat sighed. "If she can take you, then you can go."

"I still don't understand why you won't talk to Nathan anymore. He's the nicest man we've ever known. He was always good to you."

"You will understand more when you are older. I ended things because he's such a nice man. We've talked about this. He deserves better than me. He deserves someone who can give him something I don't have."

"I know, I know. That special gem thing. But I miss him, Mommy."

Kat's eyes stung. "So do I, Chloe. But when you care about someone, you always want what is best for them, even if it hurts. I am not the best for him."

"A few weeks ago, I heard you praying before bedtime. You prayed that he would find the perfect woman for him and that he would be happy. Why didn't you pray for you to find someone?"

"I don't need a man, Chloe. I have Jesus, and as a bonus, I have you, Ms. Rose, Elaina, and Mandy."

"You never want to get married, Mommy?"

"I'm not saying that. I'm only saying that it's okay either way."

Kat hoped Chloe would forget about VBS by the time they returned from the store. However, as soon as they walked in the door and she helped put the groceries away, Chloe knocked on Mandy's bedroom door, asking if she could take her next week.

To Kat's dismay, Mandy said yes.

When Chloe left the first morning of VBS, Kat's nerves were a mess. She tried to calm herself by remembering that Nathan didn't work with the children and that Chloe had grown a lot since they went there. Mandy would be taking her. Hopefully no one would recognize her. But she was still worried, no matter how much she tried to convince herself not to. She didn't want Bridgette to think she was trying to come between her and Nathan.

As Kat sat in her office, she couldn't stop looking at the clock every few minutes. VBS was from nine to twelve. Mandy was supposed to drop Chloe off at her office when it was over. Though she didn't want anyone to recognize Chloe and ask where they had been, she was desperate to learn about Nathan. How was he doing? Were he and Bridgette still dating? Were they engaged by now? But what she wanted to know the most was if he was happy. She could always ask Ms. Rose, but they had agreed not to speak about him because it was easier for everyone. Up to this point, they had kept that promise.

Chloe and Mandy walked in at twelve-thirty carrying a bag from McDonald's. Mandy rubbed her oval belly. She wasn't too far from her due date. Lately, she couldn't get enough fries from McDonald's.

"We brought you a latte," said Chloe, handing it to her with a straw.

"Thank you. How did VBS go?"

"It was so much fun! I can't wait to go back again tomorrow. I wish I could go every day for the rest of the summer."

"Well, unfortunately, that's not an option. Did you see anyone we know?"

"No. I saw a few kids from my school, but that's all. I was hoping to see Nathan, but he wasn't there."

Kat felt a surge of relief and disappointment all at the same time.

"I'm going to get back to the apartment and change," Mandy said. "I'm showing my first house in an hour. Say a prayer that it goes well. I need to support my son."

"I'm proud of you, Mandy. You will be an amazing mother."

"I couldn't be where I am today without you, Kat. I can never pay you back for all you've done for me."

Kat smiled. "I wouldn't be who I am without the help of someone either. Actually, a few someones. You can pay me back by being there for someone else."

"One of those someones is Nathan, and you won't talk to him," said Chloe, rolling her eyes.

"One day you will..."

Chloe interrupted her, "I know, I know."

"Come in," said Nathan, looking up from his computer.

"Can you go out and help with the children?" a fellow coworker asked. "Janet had to rush home for a family emergency."

"Sure," said Nathan as he stood and reached for his hat. When he walked out to the children's area, he was overwhelmed by the number of kids that had come. Shirley, the church's children's director, put him in charge of the snacks. Volunteers were passing out small bags of pretzels and bottles of water.

Nathan smiled as he looked around the room at all the little faces. They were all so unique in their own way. It was a sobering thought, knowing that each child had a soul that would one day end up in heaven or hell. He took that seriously.

As he scanned the room, he saw a familiar little face. His heart skipped a beat from excitement. "Chloe!"

Chloe almost choked on her water when she heard his voice. She ran and jumped into his arms. "I've missed you so much! I've been hoping all week that I would see you. Then on the last day, here you are."

"I've missed you too. How is your mother? Is your dad treating her okay?"

"Mommy's doing good. I don't know how my dad is. He left soon after you and my mom stopped seeing each other. He moved back to California. He hasn't even called or anything."   Nathan's jaw clenched. "So, he gets her pregnant and leaves. I had a feeling he would do that to her. Is her health good?"

"She seems to be okay. She just lays around a lot. She's having a boy. I can't wait! Now that she's gotten her new job, she probably won't live with us much longer. It makes me sad. I've come to like her. I think my mom likes her too."

Nathan gave her a strange look. "What do you mean? Who are you talking about?"

"Mandy. Before my daddy left, he broke up with her. He gave her a couple weeks to leave the house before selling it. My mom felt sorry for her and invited her to live with us until she could get on her feet."

"So, Mandy's the one having a baby, not your mother?"

"Yeah, silly."

"How is your mother?"

"She's good. We started going to a smaller church. She helps teach the five-year-olds and helps with the homeless ministry. She's also taking online college courses. She's going to be a nurse. Speaking about my mommy, I don't know why she broke things off with you. She says I'll understand when I get older. But I will never understand it."

"What does she say?"

"She says that you deserve something she doesn't have anymore. Something that was taken away from her when she was only a girl, and if she had any left, she gave it to my daddy. But if she could do it all over again, she would have given it to you. Does that make any sense to you? Because it doesn't make much to me."

Nathan remembered telling her he had never been intimate with a woman. That must have made her feel like she wasn't good enough for him, so she had broken things off.

Nathan grinned. "It makes sense."

"I know she still likes you."

"How do you know that?"

"She said it. That when you truly care for someone, you do what's best for them, even if it hurts. She said she wasn't the best for you, but she cried for weeks after your breakup. She didn't think I saw her, but I have really good eyes."

Nathan held back his emotions. It broke his heart to think she didn't feel good enough for him when she was all he wanted. All of her, just the way she was.

The teacher called the children to line up, and Chloe hugged Nathan so tightly that it gripped his heart. "I miss you. I don't know when I'll see you again. My mom's doing everything she can to stay away from you and the church. She thinks it's better that way."

"Chloe! It's time to line up," said the teacher.

As she lined up with the other children, Chloe gave him a sad look. He waved, and she waved back.

Nathan saw a glimmer of hope for the first time in months. Things finally made sense about why she ended things so abruptly and why she'd been willing to get back with Justin. She felt like she wasn't good enough for him.

Now he had to figure out how to convince her she was wrong.

Chapter Twenty-Nine

Kat jumped when her phone rang. When she saw it was Mandy, panic swelled inside her. Even before she answered, she knew what Mandy was calling about. "Hello?"

"Hey, Kat. I hate to tell you this, but I won't be able to pick Chloe up today. I just got a call at the last minute, and I'm on my way to Smyrna to show a house. I am so sorry. I know you don't want to go back there, but there's nothing I can do."

"It's fine. Thank you for taking and picking her up all week. I hope things go well for you."

"Thank you. I'll see you later tonight."

Kat grabbed her keys, hung the OUT FOR LUNCH sign on the door, and headed out. Chloe had been going to VBS all week and hadn't seen Nathan. Everything would be fine.

But what if Kat ran into him at the church? Her heart raced faster. She wanted to see him more than anything, but she didn't want to experience the heartbreak that would come after. He may want them to be friends, but that would be impossible for her; she could never settle after knowing how it felt to be held in his firm, masculine embrace. How it felt to kiss him.

Kat pulled into the parking lot and parked far away from the other cars. Her heart felt like it had stopped when she saw his car. He was here! Of course he was; he worked here.

She lowered her head and followed the other parents into the building, avoiding eye contact with anyone. She followed the signs that led her to Chloe's classroom.

"Mommy!" said Chloe as she ran to her mother.

Kat showed the teacher the picture of the matching parent tag Mandy had texted her so she could pick her up. The teacher checked both numbers. "We loved having Chloe this week. This Sunday, during the eleven o'clock service, we are singing one of the songs we learned this week for the congregation. It would be wonderful if you could be here."

Kat smiled. "Unfortunately, we attend another church, so we won't be able to make it."   "We understand. We enjoyed having her. She's a sweet little girl. Pastor Nathan seems to think a lot of her too."

The mention of his name made her chest tighten and her knees weak. She darted a glance toward Chloe, who gave her a sheepish grin. Then she focused back on the teacher. "Thank you. Chloe really enjoyed herself. Perhaps she can come again next year."

Kat took Chloe's hand, and they walked hastily out of the church.

When they walked by the playground, Kat saw her car from a distance and picked up the pace.

"Katarina!"

She instantly stopped walking. Hearing his voice again sent a rush of excitement through her entire body. She slowly turned around.

Nathan was walking toward them. His tall muscular frame beckoned her.

Chloe ran into his arms, and he picked her up. "Do you mind going to the playground for a few minutes while I talk to your mother?"

Chloe looked to her mother for her approval. Kat nodded, and Chloe ran off to play.

He stepped closer to her. She took a step back. "I bumped into Bridgette a while back, and she said you were dating. I'm very happy for you both. You make a perfect couple."

"I can see why you would think that, but I had to break things off with her."

"Why?"

"Because she's not you." He brushed his thumb along her cheek, and Kat briefly forgot how to breathe. "My feelings haven't changed for you, Katarina. I love you, and I always will."

She shook her head, dislodging his hand, and stepped away. "Please stop. I can't... You deserve better than me. I will never have what you deserve."

"What is it that you think I deserve?"

"Purity."

He smiled. "Do you know what your name means, Katarina?"

She shook her head, not trusting herself to speak.

"I looked it up soon after we met. It's why I started calling you by it. It means purity. I believe God put that name on your mother's heart because He knew you would struggle with it one day. He wants you to know that because of Jesus, you are now pure. You are a new creation."

"I know I'm pure to God, but to you I...."

He stepped even closer until their lips were almost touching. "Pure. If you are good enough to be God's daughter, then you are more than good enough for me." He slowly got down on one knee. "I don't have a ring because I didn't know I would see you today. But I don't want to live without you. I have thought about you every second of every day since we've been apart. I love and want you and only you for the rest of my life. Will you, Katarina Baker, please be my wife?"

Kat put her hands over her face and wept. He stood and drew her into his arms and held her. She buried her face in his chest, soaking up the security of his embrace, a feeling she had missed even more than she even remembered.

After a few minutes, he asked, "Are those happy or sad tears?"

"Happy tears," she whispered. She looked up at him. Her face looked the same way it had the night they first met—swollen eyes and trails of mascara streaking down her cheeks. "No one has ever made me feel as loved as you," she said softly.

He lifted her chin and looked deep into her eyes. "Katarina Baker, I promise to spend the rest of my life loving you unconditionally and showing you just how special you truly are. Will you please be my wife?"

Overwhelmed with emotions, she nodded. "I would love to."

Nathan grinned and captured her lips in a tender kiss.

Epilogue

Katarina gently bounced her two-week-old baby boy, Scott. He was named after Nathan's biological dad.

She quietly walked around the living room, enjoying their little miracle. She didn't want to wake Nathan or Chloe—especially Nathan, who had taken the first shift feeding and changing the baby's diaper so she could sleep. She only had four weeks of maternity leave left before returning to her job as an E.R. nurse. Even though she had been a nurse for a little over a year, she still found it hard to believe that her dream had come true.

Kat sat on the couch and began rocking the baby. He looked so much like his daddy, yet he had a striking resemblance to his big sister. She kissed his little forehead and tried to savor every minute. This stage had flown by so quickly with Chloe, and Kat wanted to enjoy every second.

Her gaze fell on her Bible on the coffee table, the one Nathan had given her almost four years ago when they first met. She smiled as she remembered Nathan re-gifting it to her on their wedding day. Instead of a space beside her name, it now read *Katarina Spencer*. She reminisced about their wedding day and how Ms. Rose had walked her down the aisle. Elaina had been her maid of honor, Mandy was a bridesmaid, and Chloe was the flower girl. Other than the kiss and being announced as Nathan's wife, her favorite part of the ceremony was when Nathan said special vows to Chloe and promised to be there for her.

Katarina twisted her wedding ring around her finger. It was the same ring Nathan's mom had worn when she was married to his dad.

She looked around her beautiful home that she still couldn't believe was hers. Mandy had sold it to them a month before they got married. Nathan sold his home and stayed here, fixing minor repairs before she and Chloe moved in after the wedding. They had lived here for two years and had made some of her favorite memories.

She giggled at the thought of Mandy and their friendship. Who would have thought that a person she once loathed would become one of her closest friends?

She knew only God could do something like that. Only God could have given Mandy someone who loved her like she had always dreamed. After her son, Derik, was born, she continued to go to church. After giving her life to Jesus, she met Brent, a nice man who had recently moved to the area. Now they were close to celebrating their first wedding anniversary.

Katarina saw Nathan in the corner of her eye. She turned and saw him smiling at her. "What are you doing?"

"Enjoying the view." He walked over, sat beside her, and pulled her and the baby into his arms.

"I wish you would have kept sleeping. You need your sleep too."

"I can sleep when he goes to college."

She laughed.

"What were you thinking about? You seemed deep in thought."

"How blessed I am. When I was a little girl, I never could've imagined I could be so happy. That there was someone out there like you who could genuinely love and appreciate me. You are such a good dad to Chloe. I can't tell you how grateful I am that you adopted her, and now she's yours. God has been so good to me."

Nathan kissed her. "This is only the beginning."

Chloe, with half-dozed eyes, walked out and joined them on the couch.

Nathan put his arm around her and kissed her on the head. "Good morning, sleepyhead."

"Do I have to go to school today? Scott woke me up several times in the night."

Katarina and Nathan swapped glances. "I guess you can stay out for one more day," Nathan said with a grin.

For the first time in her life, Katarina had everything she had ever wanted. She had a family, and they all shared the same last name. But even better than that, she was a part of God's family. She knew that even if she lost it all, she would always have Jesus, and He was all she truly needed.

Invitation

I think it's safe to say that you enjoy a good love story. However, the greatest love story ever told starts with the Prince of Heaven who had everything needed nothing, and yet desired to have a relationship with you. Before you ever knew Him or even cared to know Him, you were on His mind and you continue to be—so much so that He left perfection, trapped Himself into a physical mortal body, and came to this very imperfect world with nothing. He suffered horrifically by being tortured and dying in your place as the sacrifice for your sin and guilt so that one day you would be able to be with Him in His perfect world when you leave this one—instead of the alternative. He did all of this just for the possibility that one day you might choose to love Him back. It's what His heart truly desires. Whether you are aware of it or not, He constantly pursues a relationship with you.

However, the ultimate decision is yours. The love He has for you is far greater than anything you have or ever will experience in this world, and the benefits of this precious relationship don't begin just when you die but as soon as you say yes to His invitation to have a relationship with Him. Instead of fear, despair, and hopelessness, when you accept Jesus as your Savior, you immediately receive peace, joy, and hope. Although we live in a world where bad things happen, He will never leave you or forsake you and will help you through any situation that may come your way.

You may ask yourself, "How can I obtain such a treasure?"

First, you need to acknowledge and admit that you are a sinner. Like everyone else, you have sinned and aren't perfect, and you need saving. Second, repent of your sins. Confess your sins to God. Be truly sorry for what you have done that is displeasing to God. Third, believe that Jesus Christ, God's only begotten Son, died for your sins, in your place, for your salvation. Fourth, accept God's free gift of salvation through faith in Jesus Christ and His death at the cross for you. Lastly, dedicate your life to Jesus. He not only saves you from an eternity in Hell when you accept Him as your Savior, but He also intercedes for you at all times to God the Father, in order to obtain for you God's power in your life to live for Him.

Here's where you stop living for yourself (an empty life that has left you feeling only unsatisfied and always wanting more) and instead start living a life with purpose. Here is where you stop traveling alone on this path that seems to be going nowhere and start traveling with Him by your side with a beautiful destination before you—and wow, what a journey!

Will you accept His invitation? Will you make this simple choice, a choice to love the One who so loves you, by accepting His Son Jesus?

Accepting Jesus as my Savior has been the best decision I have ever made. He has seen me through the best and worst of times in my life, from the births and adoptions of my children to the death of my dad. He has been my rock. He alone truly gives me hope and joy in a world and at a time when it seems there is none. He can do the same for you. Will you let Him? This is truly the greatest love story ever told.

Believer's Challenge

Every unbeliever is diagnosed with a fatal disease called sin. This disease will eventually lead them to eternal death. If we love people the way we are called to, we must lovingly point them to the only One who can heal them. To my fellow believers, I want to remind you that God has a purpose for your life. A plan far greater than what you can imagine. We are called to take Jesus to a hurting and broken world. Luke 10:2 from the Amplified Bible says, "... *The harvest is abundant [for there are many who need to hear the good news about salvation], but the workers [those available to procluim the message of salvation] are few. Therefore, [prayerfully] ask the Lord of the harvest to send out workers into His harvest.*"

It doesn't matter your age, past, or limitations. God can use you, your gifts, and your experiences to impact a hurting world in need of the only One who can bring life and hope. There are people in your life that only you can influence or plant seeds of hope. Where would you be today if someone hadn't reached out or exemplified Jesus to you? You, too, can be that one who brings light to a dark soul destined for eternal hopelessness.

To My Readers

Thank you for investing your precious time in reading this book. You are the reason I get to do what I love.

If you enjoyed reading my book, please consider reviewing it on Amazon. Leaving a review is one of the best ways to help other readers discover my books. To find out about future books and giveaways, please subscribe to my blog by visiting my website at https://www.valeriezahn.com. Thanks again!

Special Thanks

Firstly, I want to thank God, who has blessed me exceedingly and abundantly above all that I could ask for or think. I am eternally grateful for His pursuit and for never giving up on me. He is my first love and forever will be. Secondly, I want to thank my wonderful husband Steven. I love and appreciate you more than I will ever be able to express. Thank you for completely supporting and encouraging me along every step in my writing journey. I also want to thank my amazing children. You are truly a blessing from the Lord. Thank you for your encouragement. I love you with all my heart. Next, I would like to thank my mother, Judy, and my brother Craig. This book would not be possible without you. Thank you for literally being my creative team and backbone. Thank you for always being in my corner and being there for me. I love you dearly. I also want to thank my dear friend and sister in Christ, Elizabeth Johnson. Thank you for your work and input on the invitation of this book. It's truly the most important part. Lastly, I would like to thank all of my beloved family and friends who have always loved, encouraged, and supported me. I thank God for each of you.

About the Author

Valerie grew up in small southern towns. She was blessed to come from a culture where life revolved around Jesus and family. She always had a vibrant imagination and enjoyed all things media related. As a young adult, she attended Lee University, where she majored in telecommunications. After college, she enjoyed a very successful career working as a video editor. She has worked for both local networks and a national entertainment network. During this time, she met and married Steven.

After getting married, she continued working until she was blessed with her first child. After becoming a mother, she found that her heart's desire was to be a stay-at-home mother and a wife. Since making that decision, she and Steven have become the proud parents of four biological children and two children they adopted from foster care.

While her first loves will always be God and her family, she has never lost her passion for crafting an engaging story. Her desire is to give her readers stories that will take them on an entertaining journey of romance and spiritual awakening. She hopes her writing will bring both an escape from the world's daily problems and a testimony of God's goodness, love, and grace.

For more about Valerie's books and giveaways, visit her online at: https://www.valeriezahn.com.

Made in the USA
Columbia, SC
25 October 2023

24733112R00150